A sharp clap of thunder rent the air, then an-
other and another. Sister-Major Celeste stumbled
back. Lars turned swiftly on his heels, drawing his
blade as he moved. A trio of demons stood on the
bridge, not four meters away. They were squat, broad-
shouldered creatures with powerful outsized arms,
and legs too short for their bodies.

Lars had only a second to take them in, for the
moment he turned to face them they were on him.
With a hideous grunting sound that chilled the blood,
they padded 'cross the cobbles swinging short curved
blades above their heads. Lars met the first, parried
the creature's blows and drove it back. The others
came in fast on either flank. Lars feinted at one—the
other's wicked blade near took off his arm.

Lars winced in pain and vanished. . . .

NEAL BARRETT, JR.
has also written:

ALDAIR IN ALBION
ALDAIR, MASTER OF SHIPS
ALDAIR ACROSS THE MISTY SEA
ALDAIR: THE LEGION OF BEASTS
STRESS PATTERN

THE
KARMA
CORPS

Neal Barrett, Jr.

DAW BOOKS, INC.
DONALD A. WOLLHEIM, PUBLISHER

1633 Broadway, New York, NY 10019

DAW Collectors' Book No. 604

DEDICATION

For Dwight V. Swain,
old pro and old friend . . .

First Printing, November 1984

1 2 3 4 5 6 7 8 9

ONE

He woke to the good smells of summer, hay and old wood warmed by the sun. Peppered mush and honey bubbled below, wafting tangy odors up the ladder and 'cross the loft. Of a sudden, he remembered there was business to attend; no time this morn for such pleasures. The thought brought a dark and sour mien to his face, a hollow to his belly. Tossing the robe aside, he sat and scratched, baring the pretty bottom next to his own.

"Rise and shine, Sergeant, m'pet. The day's begun again." He gave the shapely curve a friendly pat and got to his feet.

Sergeant O'Farr made a noise and covered her head. "The night's scarce over is what it is," she said glumly. "God's breath, Lars—what's got *you* up and cheery?"

"Cheery I'm not," he told her, fumbling for trousers and boots. "But up I surely am and so are you!" Catching the robe with his toe, he flipped it neatly away. Carilee O'Farr made a half-hearted grab for it and missed, yawned and stretched naked as a babe. Crossing honeyed legs, she brushed flecks of hay from fiery hair and gave him a look.

"Are you saying just what you're up *for*, or is that for me to guess?"

"Citadel business," he said. "The grand high herself, no less."

O'Farr's amber eyes got wide. "Mother Anne Marie? You're not, now!"

Lars laughed and bent to kiss her. His lips came away with the sweet taste of spice. "Of course I'm not, you nit. Y'think the virgin queen'd show Lars Haggart her face? Why, I'd seed the poor lady from 'cross the room."

"Braggart Haggart," said O'Farr. "So who, then?"

"Sister-Major Celeste. And her shadow as well, I'd guess."

"*Yeech!*" She showed him a pouty mouth. "I don't like that one at all."

"Which, now?"

"Her, or the other one, either."

"And who was it told you they were for liking? Surely not myself." Lars tied the thongs of his jerkin, searched about for his blade and thrust it in his belt.

"Lars . . . I dreamed I knew who I was," she said suddenly. "It was nearly clear as day."

Lars glanced at the wall. "And just who might you be, Carilee O'Farr?"

"Well of course I don't remember," she said crossly. "But I almost did, and that's true. . . ."

"Almost is the way dreams are," said Lars. Turning just a hair and then away, he caught the look in her eyes. Nothing at all, he decided, nothing that shouldn't be. He considered taking a peek, feather-brushing her thoughts . . . No—they were too close for that, and Carilee much too quick.

As if to prove him right, she sat up straight and raised a brow. "Now what's all *that* about?"

6

"What's all what?"

"Looks and glances and such. I'd know what you were thinking, Lars Haggart." Her head tilted askance. It was a most familiar gesture, one that made her look like a fox.

"If you know me, girl, then you likely know what I'm thinking. Thoughts of lust, and dark carnal desire."

"Liar." Her saucy lips creased in a grin. "Sister-Major Celeste, no doubt."

Lars looked solemn. "Ah, you've found me out and I'd hoped not to hurt you. Take a care now, and don't lie a'bed all day. Though it's truly where I'd like to be as well." He bent to kiss her again, and let his eyes roam free. "Lord bless me, O'Farr, you've skin as fine as cream," he said in wonder.

"You truly think I do?"

"I do and good-bye," he said quickly, watching her eyes turn to smoke. "I'll be back soon and we'll think pure thoughts."

"Now that'll be the day," she said to his back.

He stalked through the kitchen, away from pleasing smells, past stone arches and down the cool hall. A torch burned ahead and he slowed his step and stopped. Gerene McKenzie's dark-agate eyes reached out and touched him with a look, matching the whisper of sadness that brushed his mind.

"And how's our John-William?" he asked, knowing the answer as well as she.

Gerene found a smile, a poor and meaningless sham for them both. "He spoke this morning, Lars. Asked for water and said my name."

"Fine, now. That's as fine as it can be." He risked a tiny thought, and pulled away with a shudder. God's Holy Eyes—it was the same as kissing a corpse!

7

Poor John-William was hollow and dry, his mind cold and brittle as a stick. "If there's a thing you need let me know," he told Gerene. "I'll stop again tonight." He turned, then, and left, trying not to walk too quickly lest she know.

In some time past, a timber as tall as a man had been stripped and stood on end and lodged firmly in the earth. None could say what it was for, but Amian Morse put it to use every morning to scratch his burly back. It was there Lars found him, watching his troops on the training field beyond. Morse made an effort to hide the bowl of porridge and bread; a nice feat indeed as he was naked to the waist.

"You are a lovely example to the others," Lars said wryly. "They'll all be wantin' double breakfast now."

"When they get as big as me they can have it," growled Morse. He slapped his belly and squinted at the sun. "And what brings you out of your nest? Morning prayers, I'd guess."

"I'm a pious man, Lieutenant. I follow your holy example as best I can." He nodded toward the field, pinching a piece of bread from Amian's bowl. "And how are they coming along—or would you know that, standing off here and feeding your face?"

"I'd know for sure," the big man sniffed, gesturing with his spoon. "My corporal's hard as nails, and merciless in her work."

Lars set his hands on his hips and glanced across the hardpacked earth. The corporal was clad in loose green trousers and shirt to match, garments which failed to hide her abundant form. Her eyes were cornflower blue, and a shock of wheat-colored hair crowned her head.

"Merciless indeed," Lars said soberly. "A lass to strike fear in your heart."

"She's a fine leader," said Morse.

"Ah, well I'm certain that she is."

Amian eased thumbs in his trousers and scowled at the ground. "They're askin' question, Lars. There's rumors going about."

"Yes. I know that there are."

"And there's *that* to top it off." He scratched his beard and nodded at the weathered timber wall behind his back. A few torn parchments were nailed to the wood, one considerably newer than the rest. "They comin' here to watch? Is that the truth, now?"

"So they say. I'll tell you soon if it's true." He turned and took three broad steps to the wall, jerked the paper free and stuffed it in his belt. "If it is, then, just how d'you think we'd fare?"

Amian's face creased in a grin. "I think we'd scare those stiff-necked bastards out of their boots!"

"No doubt," said Lars, and gave him a proper look. "That's not what I asked, now is it?"

"No, Captain, it's not." Morse colored. "Damn it all, we're good at what we do. You know that as well as I!"

"I do," said Lars, and knew this wasn't the time to take it further. "We'll talk on this again," he told Morse, and with a nod turned and walked across the field.

A high palisade ringed the compound, rising higher still over the bare, half-hectare square where Amian's charges went through their paces. In theory, it was there to make private the Blessed Arm of God. In truth, as Lars well knew, it was another subtle touch of Mother Church fashioned to keep the Corps in its place. There was no more use for a wall than holes in a boot. No right-thinking citizen would dream of peeking inside. The simplest farmer in Jacob knew a look at the "devil's own" would sear his soul. And the Church made precious little effort to teach him better.

Lars paused at the gate and looked back. The troopers had divided into two squads of twenty—greens against the browns. Straight white lines striped the field, dotted with a hundred yellow circles. As Lars watched, the wheat-haired corporal gave a sign. Abruptly, the greens disappeared. There was a single crack of sound, as air rushed in to fill the body-sized vacuums. Instantly, the greens reappeared some twenty meters away. Most landed truly in their circles, or close enough to count. Turning quickly about, each trooper loosed a wicked bolt at his target, vanished, appeared back at the start, cranked up his crossbow and disappeared again. Meantime, the second rank advanced and fired their bolts, followed by numbers three and four. Like gophers out of a hole, thought Lars, and decided Morse was right. It was enough to send the pious into a veritable fit of prayer . . .

He took long strides up the steep cobbled way, relishing the sun against his back. The mingling odors of market teased his nose—pig-droppings and spice, honey-candy and fresh hot bread, dog strips cooking and yesterday's garbage. There were wares of all sorts, but scarce little of anything in number. It was early, but the best to be had was already gone.

Shuffling through this dismal scene was a small army of peddlers—scrawny children and wizened grannies offering beads and stones and rings, and pouches of evil odor. Each, claimed the seller, was blessed by the Living Virgin herself. Lars noted grimly that sales picked up as he passed.

"You're a poor and miserable lot," he said to himself, "a miserable lot indeed." Man, woman and child seemed cut from the same drab bolt—mean, gaunt and pinched with doubt and distrust. All wore the same duns and grays, and each stepped aside to let him pass. Some looked away, and some drew zigzag patterns in the air.

Past the alleys of Market, he could see the roofs of the town, and the stone tower of Citadel beyond. Perhaps, he mused, the Virgin herself is there this moment, watching her gray domain. And if she chanced to spy Lars Haggart, what would she make of the man? Likely less than nothing, he decided. He'd never set eyes on Mother Anne Marie and likely never would—but Lars had a fair idea she looked nothing at all like Carilee O'Farr.

Turning at a clatter to his right, Lars saw a squad of Churcher Guards pass on the double. Helms bounced on their heads, and battered armor rattled. Pikes, crossbows and wicked-looking scythes stabbed the air. Glancing north, he quickly saw the reason for their alarm. An oily column of smoke rose to the sky—at a guess, less than two good leagues from the town.

Devilish close indeed, Lars decided, and cursed his luck. On the very best of days, Sister-Major Celeste was no bargain. With demons burning farms in sight of Citadel itself, she'd be a terror for sure.

TWO

She was waiting at the middle of the bridge. There, a line of brighter stones had been set amid the cobbles, a mark that showed where sinners' common ground met the more illumined earth of Mother Church. No guards or such were needed, for no good townsman would imagine strolling past, and up to Citadel.

Lars walked to the line and stopped. Sister-Major Celeste made a circle in the air and gave a nod. "Praise God on High, Lars Haggart, and I bid you good day."

"Praise God," said Lars, ignoring the sour visage of Brother Jeffrey at her side. "A bad one this morning, I take it? And a bit too close for comfort."

Sister-Major made a face. "Close is scarcely the word. They hit us at Essau Settlement right at dawn. Haven't *touched* the place in over a year."

"Not good at all," said Lars. "What d'you think it means?"

"They're up to Satan's mischief is what it means," she said flatly. "And this is just the beginning, mark you that." She took a step closer, iron-gray eyes boring intently into his. "This is not for public ears,

12

Captain Haggart, but it's fierce worse than a simple break in the lines. They took twenty meters, held it firm and pushed us back. The Mazefield hardly slowed them down."

"I see. . . ."

"You don't, but you will soon enough. It's why I asked you here—'fore this ever came about."

"You have my full attention, Sister-Major."

Her face seemed to stiffen, which surprised him not at all. There was scarce enough humor in her soul to tickle a gnat; Lars knew for certain she was never quite sure he wasn't making light of her words. Sister-Major was a woman, but she took no joy in her sex. It was a random chance of birth and nothing more. She was a hard-eyed, wiry old soldier with a face like a dried and weathered apple. Lars couldn't imagine vital juices ever dared to moisten her loins. If, indeed, the lady was flesh and blood, her secret was secure. Black cotton robes and mail armor hid whatever lay beneath, leaving no sinful mounds to tempt the eye.

"The thing I'd say is this," she told Lars. "There are changes in the offing. Changes that will—affect you rather directly."

Lars wasn't certain what was coming. "If it's something to do with *this*—" He took the wrinkled parchment from his belt, and held it under her nose. "—If it is, then I've much to say to *you*, Sister-Major."

She waved him quickly away. "You can forget about that, Captain Haggart. There'll be no need for Mother Church to see your training."

"Good. I'm pleased you've come to your senses."

"Instead, you'll get a chance to serve us more directly, Praise God."

Lars came suddenly alert. "I hope you're not saying what I'm thinking. . . ."

"I could hardly guess your thoughts," she said shortly. "That's a talent of yours and not mine. What I'd tell you, Captain, is this. The Arm of God Regiment will henceforth take its place beside the forces of Mother Church."

"Damn me," Lars exploded, "we're not *ready* for that and you know it! Not by any stretch of the imagination!"

Sister-Major's eyes went hard. "Don't blaspheme, Lars Haggart. And remember you are being paid to serve, *not* to make decisions."

Lars saw a grin catch Brother Jeffrey's face, and stopped it with a glare. "We're not being paid, period, as I see it!"

"You've ample food and drink, as good as Citadel fare—better than any fighting soldier, by the way. And you have God's Light every day."

"Save your sermons for them," Lars said angrily, jerking his head at the town.

"Nevertheless, you will ready the Arm of God Regiment. That is an order and not a request."

"Damned if I will—" Lars stepped forward, nearly over the line.

"Captain!" Sister-Major Celeste shrank back, eyes wide with alarm. "Kindly keep your person from mine. You—you smell of lust and sin."

Lars laughed aloud. "I've no doubt I do, since I've come so lately from it. And sweet sin it was, I'm bound to say."

Sister-Major flushed. "If you're trying to shock me, Captain, you're wasting your time. God has armed me against such assaults."

"Your pardon," Lars said nastily, "I haven't had

the advantage of a pure and saintly life." He wanted very much to ask exactly where she'd acquired such a keen nose for rutting. Instead, he took a deep breath and let it out. "Look—this is a subject we could chew the rest of the day, and have gristle left for the morrow. The truth of the matter is, the Karma Corps is simply not ready to fight. We are—"

"I'll thank you not to use that—*disgusting* term in my presence," she said sharply. "You are the Arm of God Regiment of Mother Church!"

"We are what we are," Lars said bluntly. "A name can't do much to change it."

Sister-Major Celeste clasped her hands and looked at the sky. "Captain, I do my best to remember you and yours are the Holy Unborn, sent from the bosom of God Himself. You try my faith severely—though that is *my* weakness, of course, not yours."

"You don't like the service, you can always send us back. To wherever the hell you got us."

Sister-Major almost smiled. "Not *hell*, Captain. Though you're a willful sinner, for sure."

Lars waved her wearily aside. "Sister-Major, whose heaven-inspired idea *was* this in the first place? To put the Corps in action?"

"All direction comes from the Blessed Virgin Mother Anne Marie. As you're quite well aware."

"Ah, yes. And with a saintly nudge from whom? You? I think not. You've too good a soldier's head on your shoulders. Brother Jeffrey, now . . . damned if this doesn't smack of your fine hand."

Brother Jeffrey flushed. "Haggart, I'll thank you not to—!"

"Never mind, Brother," Sister-Major said calmly. "Such words require no answer. Captain, we all give the Mother direction. Nothing more than that. She draws her decisions from God."

"Ah, then it's God I need to see, is it not?"

Sister-Major went stiff. "Have a care, you are walking on dangerous ground!"

"I'd say we all are, Sister. You, because the Beelzebers are nipping at your heels, the Corps because panic has blinded your reason and you can think of nothing more but to throw us into the fray."

"That's not so!" she said hotly.

"No? And just when did God send down this wisdom, may I ask? Before or after the breakthrough this morning?"

"I cannot imagine what tempts you to put your soul in peril, but I wou—"

A sharp clap of thunder rent the air, then another and another. Sister-Major Celeste stumbled back. Lars turned swiftly on his heels, drawing his blade as he moved. A trio of demons stood on the bridge, not four meters away. They were squat, broad-shouldered creatures with powerful outsized arms, and legs too short for their bodies. Their forms were covered in thick auburn fur splotched with black; their only clothing heavy leather armor studded with brass. Pointed iron helms topped the small ghastly heads, clumps of flesh and bone with scarcely any shape at all. The faces showed no features save enormous obsidian eyes.

Lars had only a second to take them in, for the moment he turned to face them they were on him. With a hideous grunting sound that chilled the blood, they padded 'cross the cobbles swinging short curved blades above their heads. Lars met the first, parried the creature's blows and drove it back. The others came in fast on either flank. Lars feinted at one—the other's wicked blade near took off his arm.

Lars winced in pain and vanished—appeared behind the others and swung his sword in a killing arc. The blade cut air and little else. Lars stared, then realized to his horror all three were behind him again!

Sister-Major Celeste shouted a warning. Lars ducked—vanished, appeared and caught a Beelzeber blade across his ribs. He was angry, scared out of his wits. He jumped at random, coming and going as fast as he could. And always, the demons were hair-thin faster—gone before he could get in a blow, or worse still already there and waiting. They were ghosts, specters, phantoms with platter-sized eyes and terrible breath, and they could run rings around him any day.

Survival being the better part of valor, Lars ran. He jumped, popped into sight a good fifty meters away, jumped again and landed in Market. Townsmen screamed, dropped their goods and ran for cover. A dozen jumps later, he appeared behind a wall and peered cautiously toward the bridge. Apparently, the demons had called it a day. Blade dangling loose in his hand, Lars walked toward Sister-Major and Brother Jeffrey. Sister-Major's eyes showed concern.

"Are you—all right, Captain Haggart?"

"That was a fine display indeed," grinned Jeffrey. "Most inspiring."

"Shut up," snapped Sister-Major. "Get patrols out, Jeffrey—I want two companies 'round Citadel proper. Don't just stand there, do it!"

Jeffrey scurried off. Lars leaned against the bridge to get his breath, suddenly clutched his side and sank to the ground. Sister-Major Celeste came to him quickly, bent to her knees and studied his side. Dismissing the scratch on his arm, she pulled herself erect. A crowd of curious townsfolk had gathered at the far end of the bridge. Sister-Major eyed them with open disdain.

"I want water—*clean* water and clean cloth," she commanded, pointing a wrathful finger in their direction, "and I want it right now. The rest of you sinners go on about your business. D'you hear me? In the name of the Blessed Virgin Anne-Marie, make yourselves scarce!"

The citizens stared, mouths agape in wonder, then suddenly scattered and fled. In a moment, a rheumy-eyed granny left water and cloth at the end of the bridge, turned and took to her heels.

Lars grinned as Sister-Major cleared blood from his side, stanched the wound and draped wrapping 'round his waist. "Hope this doesn't taint your soul for good," he said lightly, "steppin' over the line, touching a man's vile flesh. God knows what's next. . . ."

Sister-Major shot him a chilling look. "I am two things, Captain Haggart. A soldier, and a Sister of God. At the moment, I'm somewhere 'tween the two. Pray don't let it go to your head."

"I'll try. And I'm grateful for the—*aaaaaaaah!* I—need a little room to breathe, Sister!"

"You'll manage fine, I'm certain."

Lars leaned back gingerly and sighed. "Sister, would you kindly explain just what the hell happened? The demons can't jump more than a good hundred meters—or so I've been told. What are they doing here? Their army's not *that* close to town!"

"You're right. They can't. Unfortunately, they did."

She paused and took a breath. "It's, ah—not the first time, either."

"What?" Lars stared. "Exactly what are you trying to say?"

"What I'm saying is that it's happened three times within the week. Once, even closer to Citadel than this. We've kept the whole thing quiet up to now. I guess *that's* over. . . ."

Lars shook his head in wonder. "God in Heaven, Sister-Major, if they can do that we're finished. The demons will simply—" He caught her look and suddenly knew the truth. "Of course, that's it, isn't it? That's why you've called up the Corps!"

"Yes, Captain, it is," she said dryly. "Can you stand now, d'you think?"

"I can try," said Lars. She started to help; he shook his head, got his legs beneath him, and pulled himself erect. His head was full of lights, but the pain wasn't all that bad.

"I can have two of the Guard take you back—"

"No, I think I can make it," he told her. Bracing himself on the bridge, he looked her straight in the eye. "Sister-Major, I'm going to be as honest as I can. I'm the first of the Corps to face a demon in a jump. You saw what a showing I made. Those devils are better, smarter and faster. I *ran* from them, damn it!"

"I put no shame on you for that."

"Well *I* do," Lars blurted. "God's Holy Cross, woman—can't you see it plain? We're no match for them. Not now and maybe never. I will not send my people out there to be slaughtered!"

Sister-Major's eyes went hard. "Captain, the Lord saw fit to place us here on Harmony. And, for whatever His reason, he has seen fit to plague us with these demons for two hundred years. If He wishes to test us further then He will. I don't really see what you and I can do to stop Him."

"Look, Sister—!"

"I will have new orders at your compound by the morning. Good day and Praise God, Captain Haggart."

THREE

"Damn me," growled Morse, "the bitch is a fool pure and simple. We'll not send our own out to die and that's that!" His big fist struck the table, rattling cups and spilling ale.

"Calling names won't help," Will Travers said quietly. "Sister-Major Celeste is no fool, Amian. She knows exactly what she's about."

"Then the deed's all the darker," Amian said sharply.

"Will's right," said Lars. "She knows the Corps' not ready—knew it even 'fore my very lovely demonstration on the bridge."

"Then why in all hell—!" Amian began.

"In her eyes, there's no place else to turn. It's as simple as that, my friend. They brought us here, remember—and it's not too likely they've forgotten what for."

"God's Eyes—you sound like one of them."

"Oh, do I now, Lieutenant?"

"Damned if you don't, *Captain*."

"Don't push it any further, Amian Morse." Lars slid his right leg quietly off the bench. "One more word'll likely do it."

"Lars! Amian!" Carilee had been silent so long

they'd forgotten she was there. Now, her sudden spark of anger startled them all. "Well *this* should fair solve it," she said hotly, "you two barking like hounds in an alley. By the Cross, I'm 'shamed of you both. The way I read it, the question's not an *if* but a *when*. She didn't exactly ask us if we'd fight, now did she?"

"The girl's right," Will said soberly. Taking a breath, he reached a shaky hand to fill his cup. Lars started to help but didn't, knowing Will would resent it.

Lars had long ceased to wonder what Will was doing among them. No one in the Corps knew who they were, or where they'd been before. Still, they all had a great deal in common. None were near to thirty, and most far younger than that. They were tall, light-haired and fair with few exceptions—nothing at all like the short and squatty Churchers. They could jump, and read errant thoughts. Will was close to eighty, and had no talents at all. He dreamed— wild and daring dreams that made men smile and women blush. That, and nothing more. Still, he was there, and one of them for certain. Whatever the reason might be.

"As I see it," Will went on, "the Churchers mean to use us whether we like it or we don't. Best we put our heads together and make the best of what's to come."

"Exactly," said Lars, leaning intently over the table. "Sister-Major Celeste says we'll get new orders in the morning. What they'll say I can't guess, but I mean to follow 'em right down to the letter."

"God's Breath, Lars—!" Amian jerked to his feet, and Lars warned him back.

"To the *letter*," he repeated. "Give her something less and she'll tighten the noose and choke us." His eyes swept quickly about the table. "We'll obey, and give them no cause to say the Corps's not doing its part. Good Brother Jeffrey'll be sniffing our boots for trouble. I don't want him smelling something he shouldn't."

"And what might he smell if he did?" Will Travers gave him a knowing grin.

"That we're doing what we're told," breathed Lars, "but taking God's sweet time to get it done. Buying precious days to earn just why those ugly apes are ten times better than our best—and what we've got to do to beat 'em."

"And just how long do you think they'll buy that?" asked Carilee O'Farr.

"Long enough, I hope. God knows we'll need every minute we can get."

Amian Morse looked at his hands. "I was—too fast with my tongue, I guess, Lars. Said things maybe I shouldn't."

"Yes, you did," Lars said without a smile. "You're a good man and a friend. —But don't be pushing me again. . . ."

The clouds that shaded the late evening sky opened up with a vengeance after dark. Lars lay on his back and watched lightning brighten the loft. The rain came hard and clean, a steady pleasant drumming overhead. By rights it should have lulled him into sleep, but Lars was far from that. Each time he closed his eyes there were other eyes to meet him— black and darkened mirrors come to taunt him, and with the eyes the stink of demon breath, the touch of tangled fur . . . blades keen as ice and fast as the wind. . . .

Carilee had tried to ask, as had Amian and the

rest, what was it like? How did it feel to finally meet them face to face? A dozen questions and more, and he had no answers to give. The demons were damnably good—better, faster, quicker at the jump. He'd done the best he could and fled the field. They'd laughed, then, as if it were only a folly—the Captain's jest to put them at their ease. Next time, they said— next time they'd show the devils what for.

It was the laughter that scared him the most. They'd seen what they wanted and missed the rest. *They can't feel the fear . . . they don't know what it's like. God's Holy Breath, they're eager to get in the fray . . . !*

Lars could never tell the others, but he saw the Churchers now in a different light. He'd fought the demons less than half a minute . . . the pot-helmed soldiers of the Church had faced their wrath for two-hundred years. Damn, he thought to himself, it's no small wonder they hate us as much as they do!

He knew the story well. It was mostly true, he guessed—colored a bit to fit, but close enough. The ship was one of many Mother Church flung out from their world, to lighten the burden of sinners who'd conquered the stars. The records showed where it was bound, a name that mattered no more. Between the here and the there, the ship burned up its engines and went adrift. As the Church told it now, God intended this to happen. For instead of empty darkness there was a world—a small but fertile world where no world ought to be.

With its last thimble of power, the ship brought Brothers and Sisters safely to ground. They offered their thanks and sat back to wait, confident help would come soon. —Which proved, thought Lars, they knew a great deal more about heaven than the awful reaches of space.

Help never came, but the enemy did. They were terrible to behold, and had no mercy in their hearts. The Churchers knew exactly who they were—Satan's own demons sent to put God's servants to the test. Some called them imp and some called them fiend. The name Bellzeber stuck.

That first harrowing year, the Devil came close to winning the game. More than half the two thousand missionaries died before the others learned to fight. It was no easy task, for the Bellzebers had an edge right from the start. Within their lot were those with powers darker than the rest. They could suddenly appear, wreak havoc among the Churchers, and just as quickly vanish. Not too surprising, said the scholars of Mother Church, considering the nature of demons.

Luckily, it seemed that even demons had their limits. The defenders soon learned these wraiths could "jump" no more than a hundred meters ahead. From there, they could slash out left and right in shorter hops, then wink out of sight once again. In essence, they were goblin knights of the game, 'gainst the castles, bishops and pawns of Mother Church. Why this was so none could say, but some dark cord held them back. That, or God's Holy Mercy at work. . . .

Battles raged, and swayed one way and then the other. The Churchers felled great trees, and ringed their towns and farms with sturdy forts. They were learning and learning fast. You couldn't stop a demon from making a jump, but you could greet him with a surprise when he appeared. That's what the Mazefield was for, and it took its deadly toll. It didn't stop the demons—but it kept the Churchers alive.

* * *

The rest of the story was more than a little obscure—and not by chance, thought Lars. In the reign of the Virgin Mother Anne Marie, a priest with a bent for science made a discovery of great import. He had followed the steps of his father, and his father's father before, back to a flight engineer aboard the missionary vessel. Working with ancient components from the ship—now safely buried 'neath the bowels of Citadel—he'd found a way to meet the foe on his own home ground. If Satan's imps could breach the nether regions, popping in and out whenever they pleased, could God's holy beings do less? No, said the priest, whose name was Brother Jerome. And though he'd never reveal how this marvelous feat was done, he promised the court he could bring forth beings who would match the demons' talents. These beings, he explained, were the patterns, shadows, projections or what have you, of souls awaiting further incarnation in one of heaven's astral planes. Souls, said Brother Jerome, simply resting from their labors in mortal life. Through his "God-inspired device" and fervent prayer, he would borrow a small detachment of unborn shades—draft them into service where they could do the most good.

Jerome's new knowledge nearly earned him a heretic's stake. Souls were the business of heaven, he was told. One did not simply pluck them from the bosom of God. True, said Jerome. But who could say this was *not* God's idea in the first place? Could anyone, for sure? Was it hard to imagine He Himself wished to ease his followers' burden? Possible, said the scholars of Mother Church. Very likely, added Anne Marie's Council of War, who'd watched the demons drive their armies back, one year after the next. . . .

*   *   *

When the two hundred twenty-two souls of the late unborn popped into being, they were cold, naked and afraid. Moments later, they were mad as stirred-up hornets. They had no idea who they were, where they'd come from or how. They *did* know they didn't like Churchers, or anything about them. A year and eight months later, they liked them even less.

Mother Church itself wasn't all that happy with its charges. Sacred they might be, but they were a stubborn and unruly lot. The did indeed have talents, awesome talents indeed. But as Sister-Major Celeste told Lars near every day, they were slow as Christmas bringing those talents to bear.

And *that's* no fault of ours, thought Lars, listening to the rain. What powers they had seemed to grow, sharpen with practice and time. But they were no match for the demons—God's Holy Eyes, they weren't even close!

Still, he wondered, what else was there to do? The Churchers had their backs against the wall. The demons surrounded Citadel, the circle growing smaller every day. And now, of course, there was this new dilemma to face. It fair chilled the blood in Lars Haggart's veins. If demons could suddenly jump wherever they liked—

He had no love at all for the dreary folk who'd plucked him from the somewhere to the now. Still, there was a truth he couldn't deny. If Beelzeber hordes broke through to Citadel, his own would bleed and die—as quick as any Churcher. They were on the same raft, and like it or not they'd have to row.

"Damn the bloody bastards," he cursed aloud. "Wherever I was before, I'll wager my lot was better than it is. . . !"

When he woke the rain had stopped. Droplets fell from the eaves to the stone paving below, and thunder rolled in the east. He heard Carilee slip quietly under his cover, and felt the warmth of her flesh next to his. He took her in his arms and smelled her hair and kissed her lips, and she curled in against him with a sigh. Hands began to roam, and find their favorite places, and soon they had a fair storm of their own.

Later, when she cried out in her sleep, he moved close to touch her. There was fever on her brow and 'tween her breasts. "Are you all right?" he asked.

"Yes," she whispered. "I'm fine."

"You didn't dream again, did you?"

"No. I didn't dream. I'm all right, Lars."

He knew, though, that this wasn't so, and didn't sleep again.

FOUR

Amian climbed the loft just at dawn to tell him
John-William was gone. Lars, though, already knew.
He'd felt the touch of his passing moments before, a
cold whisper of frost against his mind. Carilee woke,
and they both dressed quickly and joined the others.
Like Lars, friends who'd known the man well had
sensed his death. They shuffled quietly about, sleepy-
eyed and somber in yellow light, mumbling what
comforts they could. Lars kissed Gerene McKenzie
and held her tight, and told her he was sorry. In
truth, though, he wasn't sorry at all, no more than
the woman herself. He had seen that in her eyes and
understood. There could be no pleasure, watching a
man strangle on his dreams, fade and flicker away
like a wisp.

In a moment, he found Amian Morse, and pulled
him out of hearing down the hall. "You'll not be here
today," he said quietly. "Get someone else to put the
troops through their paces. I want you to go with
me."

"Right," Amian nodded. "What's it about then,
Lars?"

It was on Lars' tongue to say he'd larn what was

about in good time. Instead, he remembered harsh
words had passed between them, and he had no wish
to stir the coals.

"We're going up to the Mazefield, Lieutenant.
Where the demons hit the Churchers yesterday
morn."

"I know what you're after." Amian shrugged. "We've
been that path before."

"And learned precious little," Lars said flatly. "Now,
it seems we've no more time for making mistakes."
He told Amian exactly what he wanted. Morse was
to gather the Corps' best talent—a dozen, fifteen at
the most, the keenest jumpers and readers. "I'd like
to be gone 'fore everyone's up and around, so go
about it quickly and don't make a fuss. Get some
mush in their bellies, and meet me at the gate."

Amian wet his lips and frowned. "There'll be a
little service for John-William. You don't mind me
saying, they'll expect to see you there. . . ."

Lars blinked and stared. "I *won't* be there though,
will I? God's Holy Breath, Morse, you'd suffer the
patience of a saint. Would you kindly do what I
asked and nothing more. . . !"

Amian Morse stiffened, and Lars saw the blood
rise to his eyes. For a moment, Lars was certain the
man would strike him. Then, fists tight at his sides,
he turned and stomped away.

The sun hid its face behind a ragged sheet of
clouds. Lars led them quickly out of town up the
road to Essau Settlement. As ever in proper season,
the fields on either side were heavy with crops. Not
an inch was spared—oatwheat, ballcorn and vegetables of every kind were crowded one against the
other. Food was scarce, and getting scarcer still as

demon armies swallowed the land. Though the Church would never admit it, Lars knew the fields were closely guarded in two directions: One, from demon raiders, the other from hungry folk who came in the night to fill their sacks. Sister-Major was right, he couldn't fault her that—cold iron blades or empty bellies—either was a hard way to go.

The thought of death set John-William's face before his eyes. Where was he now? Lars wondered. Back where he'd been, when Mother Church had jerked them all rudely into life? Waiting, among the sleeping unborn? The thought brought a copper taste to his mouth. It was a lovely picture indeed, but he knew it wasn't true. John-William wasn't with God or anyone else. John-William was caught in the Drift.

Once, Lars had watched it happen, made himself stay to the end. She was a pretty young girl, barely seventeen. She'd caught the dream and fought it 'long as she could, then let it pull her away. Lars had watched with Sean, the girl's lover, read her sere and hollow thoughts as long as he dared. Finally, she'd cried out and gripped the boy's hand, faded like an image in the eye and disappeared. Poor Sean was left holding smoke.

The worst, of course, came seconds after that. They heard her, for a good ten beats of the heart. She called Sean's name, a cry from some far and empty room. . . .

Lars shuddered at the memory, and quickly thrust it aside. What would the good Sister-Major think of that? he wondered darkly. He'd never dare tell the Church that their magic had a flaw. If they'd brought the Corps to life, might the cunning Brother Jerome have a way to send them back—to God alone knew where? Mother Church needed the Corps, needed them desperately now. All the more reason to give them no more advantage than they had. . . .

"Well now, and where might your thoughts be?" Carilee said beside him.

Lars turned and smiled at the whiskey-dark eyes. "Why with you, of course. Where else would they be?"

"Ha!" Carilee raised her perfectly fashioned nose. "Don't waste your tales on me, Captain Haggart."

He looked at her, so fresh and vibrant and alive she took his breath away. Suddenly, words he'd never meant to say spilled free. "Carilee, you'd tell me, would you not? If you felt yourself going into the dream?"

She gave him a curious look, startled and surprised. "Is that what's on your mind?"

"It is. And John-William going didn't help. You said one night you—"

"I *said* that I was dreaming," she told him softly, and laid a hand on his own. "Everyone dreams, Lars Haggart. And not every dream is a Drift—you know that well yourself."

"Yes, I know that, Carilee."

"Besides, I'm much too mean and nasty. Whatever's in the Drift would toss me back."

"Now that's likely true," Lars told her. *I'll never let it happen,* he said to himself. *Not to you, Carilee. First I'll slip a blade beneath your breast, and that's a promise. . . .*

He led them atop the hill, a bare thirty meters from the Mazefield's beginning. A Churcher captain shot them a chilling look and made the sign. Lars looked away, pretending he wasn't there.

The ground was black and smelled of smoke. The demons had left fair Essau a charred tangle of timber and shapeless rubble. From his perch, Lars watched a Churcher brigade massed below. They swarmed about and shouted, running in a dozen different directions. To the unpracticed eye they were ants stirred with a stick. Lars, though, knew every man on the field moved with a purpose. They'd been dirt soldiers all their lives, as had their fathers' fathers before them. The drill had varied little in two hundred years, and they had it down to a tee.

"Anything special you want us to see, Captain Haggart?"

Lars turned and picked out the lad who'd asked the question. There were five men and nine women in Amian's group, most of them younger than average. "Kris, isn't it?" he said. "You've all been here before, and one time's much the same as the next. What I'd like to know today is what you *feel*, not what you see or think. Let your talents lead you instead of your eyes."

"What's *that* supposed to mean?" Carilee said under her breath.

Lars shot her a look. "If I knew what I was looking for I'd say. You're the best the Corps' got, and that's why you're here. We'll be fighting those devils 'fore long. Yesterday, I had me a taste of what it's like. I nearly filled my pants and I'd like to know why."

Half the group laughed, the others looked solemn.

"Sir. . . ." It was the boy again, and Lars caught the note of hesitation in his voice. "Sir, if we're not going to jump, how are we supposed to *feel* anything except—"

"Use your head," Lars snapped, and felt the color rise to his face. "God gave you talents, boy, do *I* have to tell you how to use 'em!"

"Uh, no sir. . . ."

"Good. I'm damn glad to hear it. If the demons show up, just sit still and listen. *Feel* how they jump. If you can, read their black thoughts."

Fourteen faces went blank. "Captain," Morse blurted, "no one's ever read a demon's mind. If can't be—" He caught Lars' look and shut up.

"*Lieutenant* Morse is right," Lars said coldly. "No one's yet read a Bleelzeber trooper's thoughts. The sooner the better." He swept his eyes 'cross their faces, saw no questions, and knew the reason why. He'd bullied them into silence, and took no pride in that. Still, they weren't made of candy and wouldn't melt. He turned and walked away, saw Carilee O'Farr and gave her a look.

"Just shut up, sergeant—all right?"

"Who, me?" Carilee feigned surprise. "I didn't say a thing."

"Good. Don't." He touched her arm and guided her off. "You don't think this makes any sense, do you? Coming up here."

"Did I say that?"

"You didn't *have* to say it. I can read your face, O'Farr. I don't have to peek in your head."

"You do, though. Don't tell me you don't."

"Not often. Maybe just a little."

Carilee sighed and brushed back her hair. It sparkled like copper in the sun. "What I think, Lars, and you are *not* going to like this at all, is that you'll do whatever you can to keep from risking even one single trooper out there. Because you know what'll happen when you do. I don't blame you for that—I

34

love you for it dearly and so do they. But you're only putting off what has to be. You can bring us up to *feel* demon thoughts, and play any game you like. In the end, though, you have to face it square. We were ripped out of heaven to fight the Devil—you can't stop that, and neither can I!"

FIVE

Her words, the bold look in her eyes, near shook him down to his boots. God's Breath—Carilee could see right through him! Likely Morse could do the same and the others as well. If he was really such a fool, Sister-Major would find him out. And when she did, she'd nail his hide to a cross.

"You flail yourself too hard," Carilee said gently. "It's no great sin as I see it, to do what your heart bids you do."

Lars gave her a scathing look. "Damn it all, O'Farr—don't start telling me I'm right. It's bad enough as it is."

"Oh, I don't think you're right at all, Lars." She shook her head firmly. "I under*stand* why you're actin' as you are. That's not the same, is it?"

"You think I should toss these people into the fray? Just like that? Is that what you think?"

"Now you know very well that I don't." she said gently.

Lars ran a hand over his face. "Carilee, I know you're trying to help. I'm grateful to you for that. But I made this stew and I guess I'll have to eat it. All right?"

"Fine," Carilee said absently. "You just *do* that, Captain."

"You're not angry, are you?"

"Angry? Why would I be angry?"

"Carilee, look—"

She turned, then, stuck her fine nose in the air and walked back to the others. He knew her too well to try to stop her. Instead, he jammed his hands in his belt and walked to the crest of the hill. The low clouds had parted, and the sun was heating the land. It sparked the dull iron helms of the troopers below, flashed off fittings of brass and the points of halberds and pikes. Lars was certain something was up. A long column jogged quickly down the road, broke to the right and headed north. Another followed, then another after that. In a moment, the columns came together far afield, three ragged serpents merging as one.

Now, a long and orderly rank nearly ten men deep faced the front. Lars shaded his eyes and looked beyond. There was nothing to see save a ruined stubble of crops, and a tumble of low hills. No doubt, the demon army was there, but they were keeping their ugly faces to themselves.

The Churcher forces waited, battle flags snapping in the breeze. In the meantime, there was a great deal of action closer to hand, for the engineers were wheeling about their mazes in some new and tangled pattern. Lars had no great love for any Churcher— farmer, soldier or pasty-faced priest. Still, he much admired the men who ran the maze. Without them, Citadel could never have held its own two hundred years. He watched with interest as they moved their heavy gear across the field. Troopers bent their backs and hauled the big timbered fences into position.

The fences were high as a man, and ten meters long. Wooden wheels groaned as Captain-engineers shouted each new section into place. The men worked with a smooth and practiced pace, butting one fence against another at seemingly random angles.

Even before they were through, workers swarmed the scaffolding like apes. Ropes were slung from one fence to the next—looped, sprung and made taut like the webbing of a spider. Armorers followed the ropesmen to lash their weapons into place. Soon, timbers were festooned with fierce ballistae, razored bayonets, and crossbow clusters that could loose a dozen bolts at a time. When the armorers left the field, engineer-sergeants took their place, reels of fine tripline strapped to their backs. Line was set to timber and looped with care about the trigger of every weapon. Lars well knew this was a job fraught with danger. Still, the men were so cunning at their craft that few lost their lives at the hand of their own devices.

Finally, the Mazenfield was fashioned, the whole operation taking nine or ten minutes at the most. It looked all the world like a fence put up by a band of drunken louts. In truth, it was a deadly and most effective trap. —Or *was*, Lars noted, until the Beelzebers broke all the rules. The trap worked on the premise that a demon could only jump a hundred meters. With the Mazefield itself a good fifty meters deeper, the cutting blades and bolts would take their toll. It was a rule near as old as the war itself: As long as Churcher troopers held the ground before a maze, jumpers were next to useless. If all that was changed, if the demons could go where they wished. . . .

"Something to see, isn't it?" Amian Morse walked

up beside him and shook his head. "Got to hand it to 'em, you do."

"True enough," said Lars.

"I don't *like* the bastards—but you got to hand it to 'em."

"My thoughts exactly."

Amian let out a breath. "Lars, you're still put out with me, aren't you? I don't want that."

Lars looked at him. "I am not put out with anyone, friend. Except Virgin Anne-Marie and her whole bloody world."

Amian grinned and squeezed his shoulder. "Damn me, I can't argue with that. I was—sort of talking with Carilee. She explained a couple of things. I'm sorry I've been running off at the mouth. I'll do whatever you think's best. I hope you know that."

Lars gave him a wary look. "Now that's the scariest thing I've heard all day. A docile Amian Morse? Too frightening to imagine."

"Well now, I wouldn't go as far as *docile*. . . ."

"Ah. Good. That's a blessed relief."

"You want to be fair, you have to say I've always said what I thought."

"Yes, I have to say that."

"Some might say it's a—fine quality in a man. What a captain wants to see in his lieutenant."

"To a point I'd say you're right."

"To a point."

"Yes."

"Meaning, I suppose, my help and well-meaning advice goes past this *point* of yours . . ."

"Amian," Lars groaned, "for God's sweet sake!"

"All right, all right." Morse held up his hands in surrender. "I push too far and I know it."

Neal Barrett, Jr.

"Just think before you speak. That would truly be a help."

"I'll try to do that, Lars. It goes against my nature but I'll try."

"Trying's fair enough," said Lars. "A man can only do what he can—God's Eyes, look! It's startin' now!" He gripped Amian's arm and pointed north, as the off-key squeal of demon horns met his ears. Of a sudden, the low hills past the Churchers came alive. Lars had seen it before, but it was ever a chilling sight. The very ground seemed to writhe and go black. The demons howled and leaped, struck iron blades against their shields and thrust ragged pennons to the sky.

At a signal, the first rank of Churchers braced their pikes against the earth. The rank behind stepped forward, covering their companions with their shields. Three ranks deep, swordsmen stood at the ready—then row after row of men with halberds, spears and wicked-bladed scythes. Last, backed against the front of the Mazefield itself, a field of archers bent their bows and waited.

The Beelzeber army came on, flowing o'er the land like dark and turgid water. Not a single Churcher moved. The demon forces roiled, closer and closer still. Lars saw a Mother Church major raise his hand. A yellow flag jabbed the air—once, twice and then again. A flight of arrows sang. One fierce volley followed another, building a bridge 'gainst the sky. A rain of iron stabbed the earth and set the demons screaming. Dark-furred warriors dropped their blades and fell away, as deadly bolts cut them down.

Still the demons came, closing up their ranks. The space between the armies quickly shrank—a patch, a thread of ground then nothing at all. The forces met with a sound that split the air. The clung of iron and the slap of leather and brass; cries of war and howls of pain and dying.

The Churcher army took the charge and held. The demons hurled themselves forward, again and again and again, but the men of Mother Church were a wall. Suddenly, a great triumphant cry rose up from the ranks. Neither Lars nor Morse could see what occurred, but an instant later the demon forces faltered, gave up the fight and turned on their heels. The Churchers waved their swords and broke the line, four-thousand men surging at once. Blades sang and slashed, cutting the demons like grass.

"By God, they've got 'em," shouted Morse, pounding Lars on his back, "the devils are on the run!"

"So they are," said Lars, though a worrisome itch touched the back of his neck. Something was wrong with this sudden rout of demons. Why would they turn and flee at such a moment? They wouldn't, he knew, not without a reason, and in that instant he saw it, a sight that chilled him to the bone. The captains just below saw it too, but it was too late to stop their men. . . .

As the demons scurried off in full retreat, their ranks opened up to let a wedge of their own troopers through. The head of this arrow fair bristled with heavy lances. Behind them came the biggest Beelzeber warriors Lars Haggart had ever seen, clutching double axes in their hands. This fast-moving force hit the Churchers like a fist, slammed them aside and kept going. Men screamed in death as iron lances pierced them through; axes sent heads flying and cleaved hapless soldiers in half.

In seconds the demons were through, hard against the last rank of defenders, now backed against the

Mazefield and fighting for their lives. Lars looked behind the demon wedge, knowing full well what he'd see.

"Jumpers!" snapped Morse, putting his thoughts to words. "Damn the devils, they've done it!"

Lars stared at the sight, a scene that never failed to bring sweat to his brow. The demon regulars charged the maze, took it swiftly and held. Behind them, the army so recently in retreat suddenly wheeled about and met the Churchers with a fury.

In that instant, the corps of demon elite reached the Mazefield and jumped. . . .

Lars' shout was lost as a roar went up from Churcher defenders. Demons appeared and vanished in a hundred claps of thunder. Triplines snapped and blades sprang free, pinning demons to timber. Crossbolts and deadly flying scythes blurred the field, cutting jumpers to meat. Lars saw a demon appear, set off a large ballista with his presence, then vanish back to safety. A split second later another appeared, in time to catch the bolt the first had triggered. One jumper wave after another took the field, but the fearsome maze held. The earth was soaked with blood, the air filled with the high-pitched shrieks of the dying.

Lars glanced behind him at his charges. Once again, the familiar itch touched the back of his neck. He moved quickly, waving Amian to him. "Get them back," he said shortly. "Off the hill and down the road!"

Amian looked puzzled. "It's not bad, Lars. The field's going to hold. They won't keep sending 'em in to get slaughtered—"

"That's the old rules, damn it," snapped Lars. "Move, Amian, *now!*"

Amian nodded, waving his charges quickly down

the rise. Lars glanced over his shoulder, heard the sudden thunder, sensed it before it even reached his ears. He ran without looking back, yelling at the others, knowing it was already too late. A furry devil popped into being. Then another and another. The hill was suddenly swarming with demon warriors.

SIX

Lars heard a scream that chilled his blood, but he dared not turn and look about. Two of the hideous demons faced him square, wicked saucer eyes dark as jet. Silvered iron winked quick and killing close, a whisper from his heart. Lars sprang away, matched the weapon's thrust and drove the warrior back. The second came at him in a blur. Lars dug in his heels, swept his sword in an arc that would cut the devil in half. Air imploded before his eyes and his blade cleaved empty space. Lars cried out as the force of his swing spun him about. He kept his balance a moment, then slipped and sprawled on his back.

Three demons appeared in sharp claps of thunder, blades cutting the ground like scythes. Lars vanished, popped into sight behind his foes, rolled to his feet and brought up his sword. Two of the furred creatures disappeared. The third turned to face him, a short-shafted axe in its fist. Lars tried to jump. Fear blocked his senses and rooted him to the spot. He saw when the blade would reach him, where it would part his skull. . . .

Suddenly, the demon went stiff, tossed the weapon aside and clawed at an arrow in its throat. Someone

44

shouted a warning and Lars vanished. From far down the hill he watched a squad of bowmen quarter the field with deadly fire. Flights of arrows sliced the air at random, clouds of angry hornets on the prowl. Abruptly, the demons quit the field. They'd faced this tactic before and knew the odds.

Lars sprang to his feet and ran for his charges, fearing already what he'd find. They were 'round the curve of the hill, below the Churcher bowmen. Amian's stolid figure loomed above them, knees still bent and a blade all but forgotten in his hand. When his eyes met Lars, Lars looked quickly away. He felt as if he'd seen a naked soul, pierced all of Amian's secrets in a glance.

Looking past his friend, he found Carilee, bent over a ruined form. Lars mouthed a hurried prayer, grateful with little shame that she'd been spared instead of another.

"How many," he asked Morse, "just the one, is it?"

Amian shook his head. "Two more, up on the hill. It happened so bloody—*fast*, Lars. There was no time, no time at all. I couldn't even—"

Amin's features began to go, and Lars clasped him tightly on the shoulder. "I know that, Morse. There was nothing you could do, so don't be thinking on that."

Amian's eyes went hard. "If I'd stayed and made a stand—Damn me, I did what you said, Lars. I got them back down as fast as I could!"

"And if you hadn't," Lars said harshly, "you'd have lost more than three and you know it. Now pull yourself together and get our dead down off this cursed hill. I want these people *out* of here, Lieutenant!"

Lars turned and stalked away, striding up the hill to thank the Churchers. Not that they'd welcome the gesture, but the bastards had saved their hides and had it coming. Halfway to the group of armored men, he saw a familiar figure and stopped cold. The spare, pinch-face visage of Brother Jeffrey peered from under a leather helm and watched him come. Lars felt the color rise to his face, and struggled to hide his anger.

"If it's you I've to thank then you have it," he said stiffly, "though God knows I wish it were any other."

Brother Jeffrey almost smiled. "Your prayers are answered, Captain. These good bowmen are not in my command."

"Good," snapped Lars, "that's a blessed relief. I'd not be owing you, and sleep tonight as well. If you'll move aside I'll find the man that—"

"Captain Haggart . . ." Jeffrey stood his ground, pale eyes intent on Lars' own, as if he yearned to bind the other with a glance. "Captain, there's ill will between us, and I doubt that will change. I can see no purpose in pretending it isn't so."

"You'll get no argument from me," Lars said curtly.

"Nevertheless," Jeffrey went on, "in all good conscience I'm bound to speak my mind. For the good of Mother Church, and you and your people as well."

"Ah, in good conscience, is it?"

Jeffrey went rigid at Lars' expression. "Yes, damn your soul, in *conscience*, Captain Haggart! I tell you now that there are—events in the making, events in which you may be offered a part. For the good of all, you must *not* let yourself become involved in—in that which is past your understanding."

Lars closed one eye. "I haven't the faintest idea what you're about, Brother. Nor do I greatly care."

"I've said too much already," Jeffrey muttered.

"The way I see it, not nearly enough."

"Just heed me, Captain."

"*Heed* you, you bastard!" Lars exploded. "God's Eyes, man—you've done all you can to turn your own people against us, to thwart us in every way. Don't you think I *know* who to thank for pushing the Corps into battle before we're ready? And do you think I don't know why? Because for some devilish reason of your own, you want to see us *fail*. Would you tell me why that's so? Damn you for a fool, don't you know if we fail then you go under as well? I cannot guess what you'd gain by that!"

For the small part of a second, Lars saw he'd gleaned some piece of the truth. Then, the mask Jeffrey wore so well slipped smoothly back in place.

"Captain," Jeffrey grinned, "if that's what you think then it's you who's surely the fool. Pray me, I've no desire to see the Arm of God tested in battle. God's Holy Witness, after what I've seen just now, you hardly fit the role of avenging angels or the—*uuuulk!*"

Lars grasped the man by his collar and lifted him up on his toes. Jeffrey chewed air like a fish, his face the color of ash.

"Listen to me," Lars said darkly, "there's three good folk lyin' dead out here, and I'll not have *you* speak them ill. Not a word from your pious mouth, you understand? Do you *hear* me plain, priest!"

Jeffrey's eyes bulged as he choked out an answer. Lars pushed him roughly away and stalked off, rubbing his hands on his trousers as if they were tainted by the touch. The man had a poison in his soul; the faint brush of his thoughts left a cold and bitter taste that refused to go away.

Lars would have given a great deal to know Brother

Jeffrey's bent—yet, he was grateful Churcher minds were closed to his touch. It was surely God's blessing Reborn folk could scarcely sense the thoughts of any other but their own. It was a truth they'd learned almost at once: that others never bothered to tidy their heads. Foul thoughts mixed with the good, and all of it floated to the top—like garbage on Ebeneezer's River.

By the time Lars reached the bowmen, they'd wandered down the hill and there was no one left to thank. He stood a long moment, and studied the field to the north. The Beelzeber army was gone. Churchers roamed the land, gathering up their own and burning demon dead. Lars could already smell their stench.

The lines of battle were no different than before, not a meter gained or lost by either side. *So what's been accomplished but a killing?* Lars wondered. *And what did I do but add to the toll?* He turned and walked away toward the others, waiting past the hill by the road.

Carilee brought him food, honey-bread and stew with real chunks of meat. He was hungry, but the first bite turned his stomach sour.

"I know how you feel," she told him gently, "but you have to eat, Lars."

"Tomorrow I do, or the day after that. But not today, O'Farr."

"Well . . . you suit yourself."

"It's not I don't appreciate it, you know."

"I know, Lars."

"You could take the stew back down," he suggested. "One of the others could have it."

"You'd rather I didn't stay?"

"Now I *didn't* say that at all," Lars sighed. "Nothing of the sort."

"Didn't have to. I know you well, I do." She turned, then, touched him with wistful eyes green and clear as polished gems. The sun spilled gold through the window, catching motes of dust and setting her hair afire. She'd donned new moss-colored leather that kissed her slender form like the skin of a willow. He could smell her across the room, the heat of summer grass, the lazy hum of bees about her hair. She asked him with her eyes, told him how they'd share a sleepy delight. He held her glance a beat, then let the moment pass.

God's Holy Breath, everything about me's touched with death, even the lovely O'Farr. . . .

"They understand, you know," she said abruptly. "They all know you did the right thing. It was fearsome, Lars, a chilling thing to face. But now we know what it's like."

Lars sat up straight. "And what's the good of that, Carilee? *I* knew that before. It didn't take three lives to say it again."

"They saw it too," Carilee said stubbornly. "The Churchers there, I mean. That's something, isn't it?"

"And what sort of something might it be?"

"Why, that you're right and they're dead wrong. We're not ready to fight. They've got to see that now."

Lars rubbed a hand over his face. "That's fair reason, and reason's no part of this at all. Can't you see that clear, Carilee? The Churchers are running scared. They've no good answers left, save to toss us into the fray. That, now, is what it's all about. Anything else is simply—Oh, Lord, girl, come here to me. . . !"

She threw herself in his arms, scalding his shoulder with tears. He'd seen it in her face, an instant before it happened. The truth of the day had found her, crawled out of the dark where she'd carefully hidden it away.

He held her until she pushed herself free, turning so he couldn't see her face. "I'm so ashamed, Lars. God, I don't know *why* I had to do that now!"

"I do," he told her. "Because you couldn't out there, now could you? You were strong when you needed to be, O'Farr."

"Huh! I was scared out of my boots is what I was."

"Anyone who says he wasn't is either a liar or a fool." He stood, then, and stretched, pulling his jerkin over his arms. "I'm going down to see Morse. Come or stay if you like. It's nothing you need to do."

"I'll come," she said firmly, "soon as I look like a sergeant again."

Lars gave her a look that made her blush. "A sergeant you are for certain, but I pray God you'll never look the part. Come when you like, Carilee. I expect Will Travers' got ale that's good and cool. I think I could face that quicker than a stew."

He was just past the kitchen when young MacLee found him, stopped him and told him he had a visitor at the gate.

"What kind of visitor?" Lars said crossly. "There's none I wish to see, and you go tell 'em that, boy."

MacLee stood his ground. "It's her, Captain. I mean—the old Churcher major. And she's got a bunch of troopers at her back."

"Sister-Major Celeste?" Lars stared at the boy. "God's Eyes, now what's she doing here, as if I couldn't guess!" He turned in a fury, leaving the lad relieved to see him go. Lars stalked outside, across the training field to the gate beyond. It's that misbegotten priest, he thought angrily. The bastard's run right to her with his tale.

Sister-Major was waiting, six stolid pikemen in her shadow, just as the boy had said. Lars stopped a meter away and glared.

"Look," he said firmly, "I've no wish to be rude, but if it's about this afternoon, I don't care to discuss it. Not now and not tomorrow."

Sister-Major looked him in the eye. "It is not, Captain, though we'll talk on *that* for certain. Now, there's a matter of far greater import." She took a step forward, looked him over from head to toe and sniffed her disapproval. "I guess you'll have to do," she said flatly. "At any rate, there's no time to change. You can brush off the hay as we go."

"Go where?" asked Lars. He gave the somber pikemen a wary eye. "I've no intention of leaving here, Major."

The iron-gray eyes bore into his. "Yes, Captain, you do," she said quietly. "Where you're going is Citadel. *With* me, and right now. For some—*reason* known only to Her Blessed Holy Self, the Virgin Mother Anne Marie wishes to—" She bit off the words, as if each were more vile than the one before. "—wishes to *speak* to Lars Haggart himself. . . ."

"What?" Lars' mouth fell open. "But—but that's not possible. Is it?"

"My words exactly," Sister-Major said wearily. "Damn you, Captain—will you *please* stop gaping and come along? Holy she is, but God forgive me, she's scarce got the patience of a gnat!"

SEVEN

Sister-Major would say no more, even after they'd crossed the line at the bridge to sacred ground. Lars could hardly blame her, for he'd scarely got his wits together himself. God's Holy Eyes, he'd be no more astonished if a band of drunken demons suddenly appeared to dance a jig! It dawned on him, then, that *this* was Brother Jeffrey's event in the making. The little bastard had known, somehow, and tried to scare him off. Which meant the pious priest was playing a far bigger part in the game than Lars had imagined.

"Damn it all, Sister," he blurted, unable to keep his silence any longer, "unless I've been deceived, Virgin Mother Anne Marie doesn't speak to, look upon or *think* about men. Much less a man like—"

"—Much less a man like yourself," Sister-Major finished. "That's true, Captain. Or partly so, at least. She has no dealings with men. Yet, in a manner of speaking she does."

Lars gave her a puzzled look. "Sister, it's got to be one or the other, does it not?"

"I'd expect such an answer from one who has no understanding of the Church," Sister-Major sighed.

"Will you have patience and listen, Captain Haggart? Her Holiness speaks to a Brother whenever she likes. But *never* directly, of course. Only through the sanctity of the Veil."

"And what's that? Some kind of a—"

"You will *see*, Captain. All in good time." She stopped suddenly and faced him, her eyes hard as stone. "What is important for you to know is that neither the present Virgin Mother, nor any who came before, have *ever* deigned to look upon a man not purified in the service of God. It is—wholly without precedent. I suggest you bear that in mind at all times."

"Right." Lars shrugged. "Very best manners and all that. And can you say just why she's picked *me* to break the rules?"

Sister-Major looked appalled. "The Virgin Mother's word is the word of God Himself. Who am I to guess why God wishes to speak to Lars Haggart?"

"Well, yes," Lars reflected. "I hadn't really thought of it quite like that."

"Doesn't surprise me a bit," she said crossly. "Apparently, Holy thoughts don't occupy a great deal of your time." Lars had a fine answer for that, but Sister-Major's words cut him off. "While we're at it, Captain, there's a matter that needs attending. I think you know what it is."

"No doubt I do," Lars said coolly, "and no doubt *you'll* recall that I don't care to speak of it at all."

Sister-Major suddenly went livid. The worn lines of her face turned to colored veins of stone. "I am your—military—commander," she said tightly. "You will engage your forces at *my* word, Captain, not upon your personal whim of the moment!"

Lars shot her a painful smile. "I wouldn't exactly

call it an *engagement*, Sister-Major. I'm afraid it wasn't even close to that."

"No, it most certainly was not," she said harshly. "God's Witness, whatever possessed you? As I understand it, you simply marched nine people up a hill, and let a third of them die. That is definitely not an engagement of any sort!"

Lars felt the color rise to his face, a shade only slightly less scarlet than the major's. His anger, he knew, was mostly for himself, for her words came painfully close to the truth.

"The intent," he said carefully, "was an observation, Sister-Major. It only became an engagement when the Beelzebers appeared on the scene. And once again, you'll note, beyond their normal jumping range."

"Wrong, Captain." Sister-Major shook her head. "This apparently abnormal behavior is no longer out of the norm. You should have guessed that yourself."

"All right, damn it, I should," Lars said sharply. "You think I don't know I sent those three to their deaths? And as long as we're passing out *honors*, by God, pin one on yourself, Sister-Major. My folk didn't have a bloody chance against those devils. We're not ready to face them and you know it!"

Sister-Major stopped under the weathered stone walls of Citadel itself. When she faced Lars again, the lines of strain and anger seemed to have vanished. "Don't you think I know the truth as well as you?" she said almost gently. "God's Witness, Captain, a fool can see your people aren't ready. That's not the point and never was. The only point that matters is we're losing—lost, unless you bring your talents to bear. Pray for strength and you shall have it. You must believe that's true, Lars Haggart. God will give you the armor you need."

"*You* pray," Lars said flatly. "I'll take the armor, and trade it back to God for another year's training."

Sister-Major ignored him. "We are late as it is," she said evenly. "I have no wish to keep Her Holiness waiting further." Turning away before he could speak, she stepped through a portal into the great stone keep. Lars followed, stopping just inside the door. The pikemen remained outside in the growing dusk. Sister-Major disappeared, leaving Lars alone.

For a moment, Lars held his breath against the silence. He found it hard to believe he was actually in the Holy of Holies itself. Only the loftiest Brother and Sisters entered here, the inner circle that governed Mother Church. Certainly, no common soldier or townsman reeking of dung had ever violated this sacred ground. According to Churcher doctrine, Holy Citadel was scarcely a step 'neath heaven itself.

Knowing this was so, Lars wondered if his eyes had somehow deceived him. All he could see were black stone walls, darkened by centuries of soot. Flickering torches fouled the air, and straw covered the worn slate floor. All in all, the door into heaven looked much like his own poor quarters—without the smell of good honeyed ale and peppered mush.

Lars turned as Sister-Major Celeste appeared again, an enormous dark-robed figure in her wake. "I'll wait below," she told him. "Sister-Captain Elaine will take you up. Try and remember where you are, Captain Haggart, and to whom it is you speak. The Virgin Mother is God's own voice in this world."

"I shall truly do my best," Lars said soberly.

Sister-Major gave him a long and chilling look. "Praise God you do better than that."

* * *

Sister-Captain Elaine waddled up the narrow stairs along the curved inner wall of Citadel. The journey seemed to take near forever, and Lars feared each gasping step might be the poor woman's last. He was certain Sister Elaine weighed a full eighth of a ton, possibly more than that.

If she falls I'm surely doomed . . . a patch of grease on the floor and nothing more. . . .

Finally, the stairs came to an end, and Sister Elaine led him down a poorly lit hall to a thick wooden door. When she turned to face him, her features were still hidden beneath her cowl. "You—know the rules, I take it," she wheezed, sucking in great gulps of air. "You do not—speak to Her Holiness. Only to—the Veil."

"And is that what I'm to call her?" asked Lars. "Your Holiness is proper?"

"Didn't you—understand a thing I said, young man? You don't call *Her* anything. You speak—only to the Veil!"

"Yes, I know, but—" The Sister turned in disgust and left him standing, staring at the intricately carven door. Lars shrugged, decided there was nothing else for it but to enter. Tapping lightly twice, he pressed the latch and pushed the panel aside.

The room was large and clean, the stone flooring polished and the rough walls plastered and painted white. A broad open window faced the west, flooding the room with light. The sun was near to setting, and the cooling fire touched every surface about with a warm and vibrant glow. Lars' glance took in the low pillowed bench, a sturdy wooden table and broad-backed chairs. He almost missed the seated figure, and when he saw her he took a step back, startled at the sudden appearance.

The woman sat so still, he'd thought her part of shadow. There was scarce little to her, a bundle of sticks all swathed in Churcher black. Her face wad dusty paper, with black holes burnt for eyes. Lars stood his ground, uncertain what to do next. He dared not speak, for there was no cloth or curtain of any sort, nothing that might be taken for a veil. God's Eyes, maybe he'd entered too quickly, before the Virgin Mother was properly hidden from his view. If that was so, Sister-Major Celeste would have his hide!

"You are Captain Lars Haggart, I suspect? Of the Arm of God Regiment of Mother Church?"

Lars was almost shaken by the voice. It was the sound of old bones in a box. "Y—yes, Your Holiness," he stammered. "I'm g-greatly honored to—"

"*No!*" The old woman sat up straight and stared. "God forgive you, do *not* address me like that!"

Lars took another step back. "I'm—terribly sorry. Is, uh—Holy Mother correct? Virgin Mother Anne Marie?"

The woman began to shake, as if some imp had suddenly possessed her. Lars didn't dare move to help. God's Witness, he wasn't supposed to *speak* to the woman without some damnable curtain between them. If he rushed to her aid, actually touched her sacred self—

Suddenly, a door opened at the far end of the room, and a young Sister abruptly stepped inside. She took in the scene in a glance, darted out of the room and came back at once with a cup of water. Bending to the still trembling form, she gently offered the drink. The old woman grasped it and pressed it gratefully to her lips, relaxing almost at once at the maiden's touch.

Lars promptly forgot the poor woman, and stared in open wonder at the girl. Hair dark as night tumbled freely over her shoulders, framing a face so fair a single glance near brought him to tears. The wideset eyes were black as a doe's, feathered softer still by a blur of downy lash. Her lips were tender petals fresh as morn, her flesh wild honey and cream. Lars blinked and shook his head to make certain he wasn't dreaming, that this fragile, unearthly beauty was truly real.

"I'm—terribly sorry," he said, his mouth too dry to speak. "I—don't know what happened. Her Holiness simply—"

The young girl stopped him with a look. Then, surprise turned quickly to laughter, a sound like water in a brook. "Oh, my . . . no wonder you upset the poor dear, Captain Haggart!" She turned back to comfort the old woman. "There now, there's no harm done. It's all right, really."

"I, uh—no one told me," Lars went on. "I tried Holy Mother, then—"

"Captain," the girl said gently, "this is Sister Anita, Veil of the Blessed of God. *I'm* the Virgin Mother Anne Marie."

EIGHT

For a moment, Lars was too stunned to speak. "But you—that can't be!" he blurted at last. "You're—you're—"

"What, Captain Haggart?" The fine point of her chin raised in defiance. "What is it I cannot be?"

"Forgive me, Your Holiness," Lars said quickly. "It's simply that— Well, I mean no offense, but you're—quite young, it would seem."

" 'Mother' will do just fine, Captain. And I'm nineteen which *isn't* all that young. And anyway, what does age have to do with what I am? How old would you have me be?"

Just exactly as you are, not a moment more or less. God's Witness, girl, I'd change not a thing . . . from the top of your lovely head clear down to your toes. Which are doubtless nibbling pink, and dear as the buds of a rose.

"Captain, are you all right?"

"Uh—yes, Mother, of course." Lars cleared his throat and tried to meet her eyes. "I was simply dizzy a moment. My—wound is bothering me some."

"Oh, dear." Anne Marie bit her lip. "I shall ask God to heal it all the faster." She moved a step and rested her hands on the old woman's shoulders. "I'm sorry you were not better informed about our ways. I fear you gave poor Anita quite a start."

"I deeply regret that, Mother."

"Oh, she'll be just fine, I'm sure." Anne Marie bent to kiss the leathery cheek, straightened and faced him again. "You do see why she's here, do you not? You must understand that while my body is here before you in a very real sense, it is—actually not here at all. Both the flesh and the spirit of the Holy Virgin Mother abide with God. Thus, while you and I *appear* to speak to one another, we actually speak through a Sister of the Veil. You can see why, can't you?"

"Ah, no. Not exactly," Lars admitted.

Anne Marie sighed. "Well it's really *quite* simple. You're mortal and I'm not. It's like fire and water. They can never come together."

"*Unless you're lookin' for steam,*" Lars muttered under his breath.

"What, Captain?"

"Nothing, Mother. Something in my throat."

"Of course you *are* the Unborn, now," Anne Marie said. A thoughtful frown creased the stretch of her lovely brow. "That's an interesting point, is it not? In a way, you're not a mortal at all, strictly speaking. You come from God's bosom in mortal form, but it's not like being—born, or anything quite as base as that. You're a soul that's risen to God and then sort of—dropped in again. Through the back door, you might say."

"I couldn't have put it better," Lars said dryly.

Anne Marie touched her cheek. "I'll have to think on this. My relationship to you is not the same as it is with the rest."

"You think not?" Lars said hopefully.

"No. Really. It's an entirely different thing. We'll talk on it again. After I've had a little time."

"I'd enjoy that Mother."

"Would you truly now?"

"Oh, yes indeed," Lars said soberly. "I—scarcely ever tire of discussing things religious."

"I am so pleased at that!" Anne Marie clasped her hands in delight. "It's my favorite subject as well." She turned, then, and walked to the window a moment. Lars watched her move with a catch in his throat. Her garment was black and plain, but there was no hiding the girlish form beneath. *God's Witness, lass, you need a gown of yellow—the color of butterflies and fragile flowers on a hill. . . .*

She faced him again, the fading sun tinting her flesh a dusty pink. "Do you remember heaven at all, Lars Haggart? Sister-Major Celeste says you don't."

"Sadly enough it's true," Lars told her. "I'm a full grown man, but I've scarcely two years to recall. In a sense, I'm even younger than yourself." He risked an easy smile, and Anne Marie returned it, a shy blush of a smile which lowered her eyes 'neath feathered lashes, and sent a surge of warmth through Haggart's veins.

"I'm pleased to see you're not angry. With me, I mean. For what it is I've done."

"And what would that be, Mother?"

"Why, disturbing your spirit's rest, Lars Haggart." She showed him a clear and steady eye. "Don't *tell* me you're happily born again. Sister-Major keeps nothing from me at all."

"Then I fear, Mother, there's been a—misunderstanding of sorts," he said gently, choosing his words with care. "Since we can't say where we've been and

61

what we were, we can't truly object to where we are, now can we? It's what you're having us do that troubles our souls, and that's the truth. Sending us out to fight before it's time."

The girl's enormous eyes seemed to grow larger still. "How can you say such a thing, Captain Haggart? It's God's will that you serve Mother Church. How can you go against that?" She shook her head in dismay. "You—you speak as if I personally wish to see men die and that's not so. I'm God's Holy Voice, not his hand!"

Lars looked at the floor. "Mother, with all respect I hardly think God wants men to shed their blood any more than you. And certainly not in vain." He raised his eyes and faced her, determined not to let her turn away. "If you're truly well informed, then you'll know we're no match at all for those fiends. God's Eyes, I'm not afraid to fight, and I can't imagine dyin's all that much—seeing as how I've done it more than once. But dying without a reason, or a say in how it's done . . . that's no better than a pig going to market."

Anne Marie flushed. "Good soldiers of the Church die every day. Are you saying I send them to slaughter?"

"They're good men," Lars answered, "and they give as good as they get. Matched blade to blade 'gainst a foe they understand."

Anne Marie watched him in silence from across the room. The dark was closing in, but there was still light enough to spark her eyes. "I see what you're saying, Lars Haggart. And though your manner of speaking's less than proper, there's truth enough in your words. Some of your folk will die against the demons. I fear I can't stop that, no more than I can stop brave soldiers from pain and suffering every day. But I *can* give you a say in the fight to be fought. I see now it's a thing that should have been done."

Lars came suddenly alert. "And just—how might you do that, Mother?"

"Why, I'll give you a seat on the War Board, Captain. Then you'll have a voice same as the rest."

Lars was near struck dumb. At the same time, he could hardly keep from shouting. "You—you'd truly do that?"

"I just did, now, didn't I? I take it this pleases you, then?"

"Indeed, Mother, it pleases me very much. As it will my folk when I tell 'em."

Mother Anne Marie pressed a finger to her chin. "Lieutenant Morse and Sergeant O'Farr. Bring them with you as well. Yes, I definitely think they should come. That'll give you three and that's fair. The Board meets tomorrow, I believe. Oh—you'll have a vote, of course. Only one, I'm afraid. Your staff will merely advise. Does that seem proper enough?"

"Very proper, Mother. My people will be most grateful for your help." *And Sister-Major will have a stroke, and poor Brother Jeffrey a foaming fit. . . .*

"It's done, then," Anne Marie said. She turned and glanced at the feeble glow of dusk. "Perhaps you'd better leave now, Captain. You've much to do, I'm sure, and it's time for evening prayers."

Lars gave her a courtly bow. "It has been a pleasure, Mother."

"And mine as well, sir." As Lars backed to the door, she took a cautious step forward. "Captain Haggart—a moment more if you will."

"Yes, Mother?"

"This—Carilee O'Farr. She seems quite pretty. I mean, from what I can see from my window. I've watched the two of you, walking to market, and strolling near the bridge. . ." She paused, then, and raised her great dark eyes. "You're not wed, I know."

God's Breath, what got her into this? "Ah, no . . . no we're not, Mother. Good friends is all we are."

"And have you lusted with her, then? Had carnal knowledge of her body?"

Lars stared, grateful the growing dark hid his expression. "Mother, what—what kind of a question is that!"

"Why, a theological question, of course," she said blandly. "One that concerns the subject of sin. You— *said* religion was your very favorite study, did you not?"

"That's not the same, now is it?"

Anne Marie sighed, a sigh so deep it caused her breasts to swell—like two young pears as fresh as spring, thought Lars. "I fear your silence gives your answer, Lars Haggart. Know that God is saddened by your sins. He forgives you, and so do I, but you *must* try harder not to err. I'll pray for your greater strength."

"Well, I can—always use an extra prayer. . . ."

"We all can, Captain. Truly we can. I know you'll scarce believe it, but even I have times of weakness and trial. I'm God's voice, of course, and thus blessed without sin and corruption. But that's a burden too, you know? Having all knowledge and—and being beyond it as well. That makes it *awfully* hard sometimes to give good advice."

"Yes," said Lars, "I can see how it would."

"I really doubt you can," she said thoughtfully. "You see, being without sin I know very little about it. I'm *against* it, of course," she added in haste. "I do know that. But I'm sometimes quite perplexed as to what it's all about. And I can see you might resent me for taking you to task. If she has no weakness of the flesh, how can she criticize temptation? That's a thought that's crossed your mind, has it not? I can't say for certain, Lars Haggart, but I'd guess sin written in The Book is simply *not* quite the same as carrying it out. . . ."

"No, I—don't suppose it is," said Lars, swallowing the catch in his throat. Her words reached him clearly across the darkened room. So did the sight of her girlish form in silhouette, and the heady smell of her hair. The scent made him dizzy and he tried not to breathe. "Well, if—if that's all, Mother. . . ."

"Good night," she said gently. "Good night and Praise God, Lars Haggart. You'll come again, I hope?" Her voice was almost a whisper. "I've enjoyed our talk so much."

"Yes, we'll, ah—have to do that," said Lars. Before he could change his mind, he opened the heavy door and slipped through. Pausing a moment to catch his breath, he hurried down the narrow stairs, taking the steps four at a time.

Sister-Major waited below, torchlight turning her armor pewter-gray. When Lars appeared she straightened, taking him in with a cool appraising air. If any silver's missing, said her eyes, we'll know exactly where to look.

"Well, you were up there quite a while," she said flatly. "I trust your audience went well?"

"Oh, quite well," said Lars. "I was most impressed with the Holy Mother."

"The Virgin Anne Marie's a saint, Lars Haggart.

You're a most fortunate man. Even a moment in her presence is a blessing."

"Oh, it's all of that," said Lars.

"You were proper in your manners, I hope. God's Witness, if you weren't—"

"Sister-Major!"

"Huh! And what did Her Holiness have to say?"

"That's a sacred thing to me. I wouldn't care to share it."

"Don't go pious on me," she said sharply. "I know you too well, Captain!"

"Do I ask what God says to you? Do I now, Major?"

Sister-Major made no effort to hide her disgust. "I've brought two guards to see you back. They'll light the way as far as the bridge."

"Ah," sighed Lars, "back to tainted soil. After the glories of Citadel, to be cast once more into the pit."

"Go on," Sister-Major said firmly, " 'fore *I'm* too tainted to say my prayers. The War Board meets tomorrow, by the way. I should have news for you after that."

"Perhaps we'll talk again, even before." Lars grinned.

"What's that?"

"Nothing at all, Major. Praise God and good night." He slipped out the portal, and found the pikemen by the wall. When they'd gone a few steps down the hill, he stopped and glanced up, in case the Holy Mother might be standing at her window in the dark. For a moment, he was certain he saw the pale reflection of a face. Still, he decided, it might have been good Sister bag o'bones the Veil, a trick of the light, or maybe nothing at all.

NINE

Lars could feel their presence long before he reached the gate—the soft humming sound about his head, a tingle on the surface of his skin. Somehow the word had spread, and the whole Corps was waiting. They knew where he'd been and who he'd seen. No one had to tell them, they simply knew.

"Yes," he said at once, "I've seen her," raising his hands above the crowd. "I can't answer all your questions. I'll know much more on the morrow."

"Do we fight, Captain?"

"Will she send us out, Lars? Do we face the demons still?"

"What's it to be, Captain? Tell us that at least!"

"Yes," Lars answered, "we'll be facing demons soon. I fear there's no changing that. But now, at least, we've a hand in the matter ourselves. A voice on the War Board itself. And that, my friends, is a hell of a lot more than we had!"

They cheered him loudly at that, and Lars took the moment to break through the crowd, motioning Amian to him, and Carilee and Will.

*　　*　　*

"It's true what you told 'em?" Amian asked, passing Lars a cup of cooling ale. "She told you that herself?"

"She did," said Lars, "but it's not as grand as it seems, friend, if you'll think on it a moment." Amian raised a questioning brow, and Lars wiped foam from his mouth. "Look," he said, letting his eyes touch them all, "we've seats around a table, and only a single vote. There's what, now—maybe eight or ten others on the Board? Can you picture a Churcher siding with one of us?"

Amian's mouth twisted under his beard. "You put it like that," he growled, "it doesn't amount to much. I don't see we're gaining a thing at all."

"I wouldn't say *that* now," chimed in Carilee.

"You told them a bit of truth out there," said Will. "It's more than we had before. But I don't think a seat on the Board's the true gain, any more than you do yourself. The ear of the Holy Mother is what we've won, and *that* could be a fair prize indeed."

Lars nodded grudging agreement. "It could be, Will, you're right enough in that. Whether it's so remains to be seen."

"Well I'd say Will's right as rain," blurted Morse. "God's Eyes, Lars—she's running the show, is she not? They've got to do what she tell's 'em!"

Lars tried to hide his irritation. That was the problem with Amian Morse, he bounced like a ball from one speaker to the next. The last word he heard was the one he believed—he never seemed to think about chewing the matter himself.

"It's not quite as simple as it seems," Lars explained. "She's the Holy Mother, Morse, and head of the Church for sure. But she's also a slip of a girl, young and sheltered and shut off from the world. All she sees are bloody priests and old women."

"They use her, then," Will said softly.

"I'd be damn surprised if they didn't, wouldn't you? From what I saw, the lass'd be no match for Sister-Major—or the good Brother Jeffrey himself."

"Yet, this *poor* lass somehow got the idea to call for you," Carilee said wryly. "Who d'you think put *that* fine thought in her head?"

It was a question Lars had already asked himself. And, incredible as it might seem, he thought he knew the answer—that the idea was wholly her own. It almost had to be. What good Churcher would find such a meeting less than appalling? Somehow, she'd gotten it into her head she wanted to see Lars Haggart. Why, was something he didn't care to examine too closely at the moment. All that talk of carnal lust and such. Damn it all, the way she'd caught his eye that once—

"I can't really say," he told Carilee, suddenly less than anxious to meet her glance. "It's a question that bears some thought."

"I'll say it does," said Carilee.

Without a word she left him, coming to her feet and padding softly across the loft. For a while she stood in silence before the window, naked to the night and the touch of the moon. Lars watched her, marveled at the beauty of her form, the way pale and dusty lemon light stroked her flesh.

She waited but a moment, then bent to retrieve her robe and wrap it tightly about her shoulders. "Now why'd you do that," Lars complained. "You're a wonderful sight to see, Carilee."

"Am I now, Lars? It's fine of you to notice such a thing."

He came to his knees at once, alert to the sudden

edge in her voice. "Carilee, what's wrong? Come here and tell me what it is."

Carilee didn't move. "Why, it's nothing that I can see. What could be wrong, Lars Haggart? That was very fine loving, was it not?"

"It was for certain. Better than ever, I'd say. So what's got you—"

"Better than ever, you think?"

"Why—yes, I'd say it was. What's wrong with that?"

"Not a thing." She shrugged, tossing a veil of hair about her throat. "What could—*possibly* be wrong with good loving? Especially if it's—truly better than ever, as you say. . . ."

"Damn it, now," he said irritably, "whatever game you're playing, will you stop it right now? Say what you want to say, Carilee."

"Is she very pretty, Lars?"

"What?" The question took him off guard. "Why— who is, love?" He tried a laugh that went hollow in his mouth. "You don't mean the Holy *Mother*, now do you?"

"I mean," Carilee said coolly, "that poor little lass, that slip of a girl sittin' lonely in Citadel."

"Oh, for God's sake, O'Farr. . . ."

"Ah, yes, O'Farr," she mocked, "don't be a fool now, O'Farr. *Damn* you, Lars, *answer* me! Is she pretty or is she not? Suddenly, this Churcher *hag* in the tower's not all she seems to be!"

Lars was shaken by the power of her anger—anger that sparked her eyes across the dark, and lashed out at his mind with sudden fury.

"She's—not unpleasant in appearance," he said. "I wouldn't say she's that."

"Not unpleasant."

"No, not really."

"A shade this side of ugly, would you say?"

"Carilee, the girl's pretty enough, all right. I was, uh—quite surprised, I'll admit. I mean, seeing as what she is. God's Breath, what *difference* does it make? It's the Virgin Mother we're talking about, remember? What's she got to do with us? Damn me, now, she's no more notion of a man and a woman together than—than—"

"*Stop it!*" Carilee screamed. Her whole body trembled, and the force of her mental rage shrieked about him like a storm. "What do you think I am, Lars Haggart? I was there, my body one with yours, and it *was* finer than ever. God, was it fine—fierce and lovely and wild as it could be. And I kept wondering, Lars, just when your bloody *mind* would enter me as well. When I'd feel you there as ever, your thoughts tanglin' with mine with a heat so strong it was fair close to dying. Damn you, Lars, how could you? *How could you make love to her, and use my body to do it!*"

"Carilee, listen—"

She was gone before he could bring the words to bear, down the ladder and gone, leaving the sound of her sobbing in her wake.

He sat up straight as the terrible din reached his ears. Cursing under his breath, he stumbled to the window and stared, jerked on his trousers and scrambled down the ladder. The others were standing about, huddled in sleepy groups against the first light of the day. From the far side of the palisade wall came the shouts and angry chants of gathered townsmen—plus a steady stream of offal, rotten cabbages and overripe melons. Lars stepped quickly aside as something foul splattered a few meters away.

"Bless me now," Amian's hearty voice suddenly blurted out of the dark. "It's a fine celebration in our honor, I do believe. This is the stuff the bastards eat for breakfast!" His words broke the tension and spread laughter through the crowd. Lars silently thanked him for that.

After a good ten minutes, the sound of marching boots reached their ears. Moments later Churcher soldiers cleared the streets, and all was silent again.

"The faithful up in arms, Lars Haggart. An inspiring sight to see."

Lars turned to find Will Travers at his side. "You hear what they were shouting? I couldn't make it out."

"Devils living among us," shrugged Will. "God strike dead the Unborn . . . Save our Holy Mother from the Beast. That's you, I'd guess. So who you figure put 'em up to it, then? This misbegotten lot'd never dare such a thing on their own."

"Hard to say," said Lars, though he'd bet his tainted soul he knew the answer. Brother Jeffrey's greasy thumb was in the soup, stirring up trouble as best he could. The man was starting to irritate Lars no end.

"None of my affair," muttered Will, "but Carilee came crying to my room, and spent the night with me."

"Well you old devil, Will. And flaunting it in my face."

"Huh!" Will growled, "not what I meant at all, and you know it. God's Eyes, that's the worst part of not remembering who I am and what I was. You know? I can't even recall how it felt beddin' a woman. Though there's feelings still there, and I know I must've loved a few in my day."

"None of us came here with memories, Will. The past is the same for us all."

"Like bloody hell it is," snapped Will, giving Lars a nasty look. "You and the rest can take your pleasure, and make new memories every night. I'm way past that, for certain!"

"Sorry," Lars said contritely, "I guess I wasn't thinking too clear."

"Don't have to tell me that," said Will. "Any man who'd send O'Farr out crying in the night isn't thinking much at all."

Lars wondered if the day could get much worse and decided it could. Amian Morse was surly as a bear, snarling at the pikemen who'd come to take them to Citadel. Carilee O'Farr wouldn't deign to glance his way. As far as she was concerned, Lars simply didn't exist. And to make matters worse, she'd never looked lovelier in her life. Her wide eyes sparkled and her skin fairly glowed. A fiery tumble of hair crowned her head in disarray, and her clothing clung to her like a dew. Lars couldn't decide whether she walked like a queen playing a tart, or a tart with her eye on the throne. It was all the stern-faced Churcher guards could do to keep from stumbling over their boots. A fine trio we are, he thought darkly. They'll likely lock us up 'fore we ever get to the bridge.

Sister-Major was waiting outside the keep. The storm doing battle in her eyes told him all he needed to know. She was furious, ready to run him through where he stood. Lars sighed, confident the day would continue to go downhill.

"God's Witness, Captain—!" She pulled him aside from the others and brought her leathery face up to his. "You could have told me, you know. You—you *deliberately* kept it from me, damn your soul!"

"What, now?" Lars shrugged, thoroughly enjoying the woman's discomfort. "What is it you're saying, Sister-Major?"

"I am talking about your blessed *appointment*, Captain. And don't play the fool with me. I'm in no mood for it now!"

"Come, now," said Lars, "I'm only a simple soldier, and you're one of the masters of Citadel. I never dreamed you didn't have the Mother's ear."

"Lars Haggart, I'm warning you plain . . ." The already livid features turned a shade closer to black. Then, as quickly as it had come, the storm floundered and died. "I—don't know why I bother," she said wearily. "I'm one of the few friends you've got in Citadel, and you're too proud and foolish to see the truth."

Lars looked at her. "That's where you're wrong, now. I don't much like you—but for some peculiar reason I half trust you, Sister-Major."

"You have a strange way of showing it, Lars Haggart."

He studied her a moment, and decided to jump right in. Though he hated to admit it, he could no longer stand apart from the intrigue of Citadel. He was, in effect, what a great deal of the scheming was all about. Best, then, that he pick a side he could stomach and stick to it.

"All right, then, I'll show you where I stand," he said firmly. "If you'd wanted to know the Virgin Mother's plans, you should have asked your very dedicated aide, Brother Jeffrey. *He* knew all about it, for sure. Yesterday on the hill after the battle. He warned me to stay away from an *offer* coming my way. That I'd regret getting involved if I did. As I see it, Mother Anne Marie made the offer, and that's why I'm here. Now how did Jeffrey know—and why didn't you?"

Sister-Major stared, then laughed out loud. "Nonsense, Captain. Don't play me the dunce again. Trying to turn me 'gainst my own is no way to show your trust."

Lars shrugged. "Fine, then. You ask for a token and now you have it. Think on it awhile, 'fore you tell Brother Jeffrey what I said."

Sister-Major shook her head. "If Jeffrey were a schemer, Lars Haggart, he'd not put such a weapon in your hands."

"And why would he not?" Lars asked blandly. "He'd know you'd not believe me. And he'd be right, would he not?"

Sister-Major gave him a look as if he'd been a naughty child. "Best you stick to your blade, Lars Haggart. I don't think you've the head for palace plots." She turned and stalked away, leaving him with Carilee and Morse. Lars couldn't help but admire her. The iron-gray eyes revealed nothing she wished to hide. To save his soul he couldn't guess whether she believed him or thought him a fool.

TEN

"There is no question at all on the matter," the old man said stubbornly. "I'll quote from the Holy Book if you like."

"That won't be necessary, Brother Ezekiel," Sister-Major said politely. "Your point is certainly well taken."

" 'Yea, I say unto you,' " Ezekiel droned on, " 'in those days unclean spirits walked the earth, serpents clothed in the manner of men and bearing great swords that spake with fire. And lo, from the darkest pits came jackals and other foul beasts. . . .' "

"Your pardon," another old priest broke in, "but I do fear you've erred, Brother. The word translates more precisely as *wolves*, not jackals."

"Brother, it surely does not," Ezekiel snapped. "Why, it would change the whole meaning of the passage!"

"Of course it changes the meaning, and that's the point. A jackal is *not* the same as a wolf. Thus, the prophecy tells of a battle in the past, not one that's yet to be fought."

"Foolishness," Ezekiel scoffed. "That's all clearly defined in verse four, if you had the sense to look.

'And unto Satan came beasts as yet unnamed, furred and feathered and scaled, of hoof and claw and talon.' *Unnamed*, you see? That's what the prophet wishes us to know. It means the beasts to come are those we cannot see, because they've yet to appear. A day, then, an event that's still to come. 'Verily, Satan stood upon the mountain and counted his legions below. First came the lions, three upon a score, then carrion birds that clouded the sky . . .' "

God's Eyes, Lars thought wearily, *if this is a council of war strike me dead. It's an old mens' bloody talkin' contest is what it is!*

The two old priests had droned on for nearly an hour, and showed no signs of slowing down. Lars glanced across the table at Sister-Major. Clearly, she'd faced the problem before, and mastered the art of looking alert while her thoughts roamed somewhere else. Two of the older Sisters were plainly asleep. One ancient Brother hadn't moved since Lars had entered the room. Lars wondered if he'd died—and if he had, when anyone would notice.

The War Board members were very much as Lars had expected. Besides Brother Jeffrey and Sister-Major, there were seven stern and sour-visaged folk, haughty pinch-faced Churchers and not a friendly eye in the lot. Despite attempts at splendor, their priestly robes and armor left them shoddy at the best, near as colorless and drab as common townsmen and men-at-arms. *Damn me*, thought Lars, *the war's gone on too long. A bit more time and these folk'll simply rot, and scarce even notice the demons have won.* . . .

"Jackals plain enough," Ezekiel insisted. "Why, it's clear as can be, Brother!"

"You wouldn't know *clear* if it hit you in the face," the other muttered. "Your brain's so muddled now you can't—"

"What! What!" Ezekiel's spindly frame shook and his face began to purple. "Muddled, is it? Muddled, you say?"

"Muddled, muddied, clogged with lint and waste...."

" 'And lo,' " Ezekiel shouted, " 'false prophets shall arise and befool their betters!' "

"You old fool, that's not in the Holy Book and you know it!"

" 'Yea, and God shall smite them down, one by one, until His word is—' "

"Damn it all, enough!" Lars stood abruptly, sending his chair clattering against the wall. "I didn't come here to listen to sermons, I came to talk about *now*. What's happening out there—" He jabbed a finger north and swept his eyes about the table. "You want to put my folk in battle I guess we'll fight. But we'll by God *talk* about it, 'stead of babbling out of a book!"

Brother Ezekiel shrank back, staring at Lars with wide-eyed disbelief. At once, the other councilors rose and shook their fists, shouting at Lars in pious rage. Some made the sign against evil in the air.

"Stop it, all of you!" Sister-Major's parade-ground bellow drowned them out. At once, her iron-gray eyes bored into Lars. "*Sit down, Captain Haggart, and do it now* . . ." Lars retrieved his chair and sat. Sister-Major took a deep breath. "I must apologize for our esteemed new *member*," she said dryly. "He is clearly not accustomed to our ways." She shot Lars another warning look. "Understand, Captain Haggart, that Brother Ezekiel and Brother Jacob were indeed discussing the war. All things past and present and those to come are writ in the Holy Book. One must simply have the faith to seek them out."

"And the will to stay awake," Amian muttered under his breath next to Lars.

Lars kicked him hard beneath the table. "Well, then, I do pray for forgiveness," Lars said testily. "Would one of you prophets tell a poor ignorant sinner how the next battle will fare? And how many folk I'll lose? I'm sure it's there somewhere in the Book."

There was a sharp intake of breath about the table. "*Blasphemer!*" hissed an ancient Sister. "You're Satan's own, sure as the Sign!"

Lars laughed in her face. "Doesn't it strike you as passing strange, Good Sister, that the Holy Mother Herself would place a devil on your Board? Since she's God's own Voice, it's His will that I'm here. Unless, of course, Her Holiness made a *mistake*. That can't be what you're saying, now is it?"

The Sister's eyes went wide, and the color drained from her face.

"That'll be enough, Lars Haggart," Sister-Major said between her teeth. "You were placed here as you say, by the Holy Mother's order. You have a vote and you have a voice. Do *not* take that to mean that you'll now be running Mother Church itself."

"I wouldn't dream of trying," Lars sighed. "I'd simply like to hear about the present instead of the past. The War Board *does* discuss such matters, at one time or another?"

Sister-Major ignored his taunt. "The War Board's purpose is to *clarify* the theological basis of the war, Lars Haggart. Then I, along with officers such as yourself, carry out these findings in the field. We *interpret* the word of God, as it were, in a military manner." She paused, then, and spoke to him clearly with her eyes. "Does this aid in your understanding, Captain?"

"Yes," Lars said soberly, "it does. Thank you, Sister-Major." Her look told him nearly as much as her words, and Lars felt fully rebuked. *If you'd told me of this appointment*, she was saying, *then I'd have told you what the War Board's all about, you damned fool!*

"Good," Sister-Major said firmly, "then we can get about our business? Ah, Brother Ezekiel?"

"Sister-Major," an elderly priest spoke, "just one thing, if you will?"

"Yes, Brother Job?" Lars caught the slight hint of tension in her words. "You—had something to say?"

The old man rose, and bowed slightly in Lars' direction. Lars noted he was seated next to Jeffrey. That Good Brother hadn't glanced in Lars' direction even once, and made a special point of avoiding him now.

"I must say that I do *not* countenance your behavior here, young man," said Job. "But in all fairness I'd say a word. A shameful thing happened this morning, and none of us have spoken of it yet. Our townsmen behaved badly. We owe you an apology for that, Captain."

"Why, uh—well, thank you," said Lars. The old priest's words took him totally by surprise. From the shocked looks of the others, they were no less startled than he. *An apology from Mother Church? God's Witness, what next!*

"That's very appropriate," Sister-Major said quickly, "very appropriate indeed. Now, if we can—"

"—And further," Job went on, as if Sister-Major didn't exist, "I think we should let Captain Haggart and his friends know our fervent prayers go with them."

"My thanks again," said Lars.

"Tomorrow, when the Arm of God Regiment goes forward to meet the foe, I am certain you'll do your best."

"Well, we'll surely try to— Huh? What's that?" Lars came to his feet again. "When we do *what* tomorrow, priest? By God, what's about here!" His gaze turned swiftly on Sister-Major. One look and he cursed himself soundly for a fool. Only a moment before, understanding had passed between them. Now, he knew she'd slyly taken him in. "Well now, this was to be a surprise, was it, Major? And it's not even my birthday, far as I know."

Sister-Major flushed. "This is a matter we'll take up later, Captain Haggart."

"Oh, no. We'll discuss it here and now," Lars said firmly. "This is a *War* Board, is it not? Then by God, let's talk about war." He looked about the table, and gave them all a nasty look. "My, it's fine to be a full votin' member of this cozy little group. Keep your ears open, you might learn when you're going to die. *Damn* the lot of you bastards!" His big fist came down hard and shook the table. "Just when were you going to tell us? Before or after breakfast?"

"Captain, please—" Sister-Major shouted, "it is *not* like that at all!"

"God's Eyes, I'm betting I know exactly what it's like!"

"Then you'd be dead wrong, you young fool."

Lars laughed. "There, now. *Dead's* the right word, I won't argue that." He turned and let his eyes sweep the table. "How did you plan to spend us," he said sharply. "Could you tell a fellow member of the Board?"

"Lars Haggart, you—"

"I didn't ask you," Lars bellowed, "I asked *them!* You—" He poked a finger at Brother Ezekiel. "What's it say in the Book, priest?"

The old man hesitated, then wet dry lips and came to his feet. "It is—writ in the Book for all to see, young man. There's, ah—no reason you shouldn't hear." Sister-Major rolled her eyes to the ceiling. Brother Ezekiel flipped a few heavy pages. "Ah, yes. . . . 'And lo, Satan shall face them with his hordes, and God shall fling a legion of his angels into the fray . . .'" Ezekiel looked up. "There—you have it clear as glass."

Lars' eyes narrowed. "That's supposed to be an answer? And which is the Karma Corps? Satan's hordes or God's angels? I can never keep us straight. . . ."

A collective gasp circled the table. Brother Ezekiel took a breath and jabbed a finger at the page. "The Holy Book says it plain. 'God shall fling a legion of his angels into the fray.' How else, now, would He Fling but with his heavenly arm? And who but the *Arm* of God Regiment of Mother Church?"

"Praise God!" Brother Job shouted, and the other members promptly echoed his cry.

For an instant, Lars felt his knees turn to water. Then, fury gripped him again and he turned on Sister-Major. "My God," he said in wonder, "*all* of us then, is it? You worked it out among you, and never intended to let us know. You'd send us out untried and watch us die. Because some simpleminded priest thinks he saw it in a book!"

"Nay, not to your deaths," Ezekiel cried. "The

Book is clear on that. 'Yea, the legions of God shall sweep His enemies from the field. The heavens shall resound with God's glory!' "

"Not if I can help it, they won't," snapped Lars. "*You* sweep the bastards from the field, old man. I'll not send my folks to die and that's that!"

"You will obey orders, damn you!" Brother Jeffrey suddenly stood, his eyes over-bright with righteous fire. "If you dare defy Mother Church—"

"You'll what?" Lars laughed. "Condemn us to death, Brother? By the Sign, you've already done it. Amian, Carilee— We're leaving this pesthole now, and not by the door!"

Brother Jeffrey shouted. His words were lost in the sharp explosion of air as Lars Haggart vanished. An instant later, Amian and Carilee followed. Two Good Sisters and a Brother fainted dead away. Another, Brother John of the Path, swore to all later he'd heard devilish laughter, and smelled the odor of brimstone in the air.

ELEVEN

Late in the afternoon, Amian Morse came down from the roof and searched out Lars and Will Travers. "They're still movin' up troops," he reported, "and plenty of 'em, too. North and west of the Essau field. They weren't lying about a battle."

"No, I didn't think they were," said Lars. "Everything else, most likely, but not that."

"Looks to me like they're sending up everything they've got," Amian added. "Second-line archers and town pike reserves. Something big's brewing."

"Good," Lars said darkly. "They've plenty of meat to throw in the fray, and they don't need us." He looked steadily at Morse. "That's all, then?"

"Uh, yeah, I guess it is."

"Then what are you waiting for, man? Are you planning on putting down roots?"

Morse colored and puffed up like a toad, then turned on his heels and stomped off. Will Travers picked his teeth with a straw. "Feels good to spit in a man's face, I always say. Takes your mind off your troubles."

"All right, Will. . . ."

"Sometimes, of course, a man'll remember such a

gesture. Say, at the moment you need him most, when you—" Lars turned on him, his eyes slivers of glass. "Go on, say it," said Will, giving his captain no ground. "That'll make it three, will it not? Carilee, Amian and me. Who were you thinkin' on next, Lars Haggart?"

Lars looked past him, through the narrow window into the heat. "I don't know," he said dully. "Who do you suggest?"

"What *I'd* suggest is what you don't want to hear. Get off your rear and go and talk to the old witch." Lars made a face and Will grinned. "You've made your point, boy. She can see our crossbows bristlin' and the message is clear. Try and take us and we'll fight—right down to the last brave lad and slip of a girl. She knows what you're saying—now it's time to talk."

"Damn it all," Lars said crossly, "what's the good of that?"

"I've no idea at all." Will shrugged. "What's the good of sittin' here?"

He walked across the hard-baked field to the palisade wall and called to the Churchers he was there. This last was only a gesture, for he'd seen half a hundred pot helmets take a peek, then vanish out of sight. She was there, he was certain, waiting for him to show. Still, she kept him standing—just long enough and no more.

"Well, are you coming out or am I coming in?" she called through the gate.

"I'd prefer to play the host," Lars said coolly, "if it's all the same to you." Without waiting for an answer, he slid the heavy bolt, opened the gate enough to let her in then slammed it fast again.

Sister-Major looked him over. "Do we stand out here in the heat, Captain Haggart? I could use a cup of ale if you have it."

Lars looked amused. "Ale now, is it? What's the world coming to?" Sister-Major ignored him. She stalked to the shady side of the barracks and plopped herself down on a bench. Lars went inside and returned with copper mugs. Sister-Major took a long healthy swallow, touched her lips with the edge of her habit and sat back.

"I'll cut through a lot of useless talk if you like," she said flatly. "There's no use wasting time, me saying what I think of you, and you doing the same. Agreed, Captain?"

"A wise idea, I'd say."

"Good. We've been trading abuse for two years, Lars Haggart. I say we'd better stop. Time's precious short and we can't afford it. You should have warned me Mother had named you to the Board. I'm not surprised you didn't. In your boots, I'd likely have done the same. Still, if I'd known I could have done things different. I did *not* betray you, Captain. I ask that you believe me on that. I meant exactly what I said in that room. The Board decides what The Book has to say. *I* decide how it works. I had no intention of tossing your whole regiment to the demons. God's Witness, why would I? What would be the purpose?"

"Then you should have told me that," Lars said darkly. "Outside, before we went in. Before that bloody priest opened his mouth."

"Good Brother Job?" Sister-Major considered her words a long time. "I never thought I'd live to see it but here it is, Lars Haggart. We're allies, you and I, whether we like it much or not. We'd *better* be, or we'll perish. And that's the God's own truth." Her iron-gray eyes seemed to look right through him. "I'm shamed to say it, Captain, but what you guessed is true. Brother Jeffrey's against me, determined to bring me down. Warning you *not* to see the Mother was a dare—a taunt that was meant for me. He's throwing it in my face, telling me he's strong enough to move."

"And is he, then?"

"Oh, yes," she said dryly. "He has the power, and I'm certain he means what he says. He'll try, all right." She paused and looked curiously into her cup. "Brother Job, now. You see what that's all about? Job's in Jeffrey's pocket, along with some of the others. Some I know about and some I don't. Jeffrey knew I didn't want you told they'd committed all your folk to one great battle. He knew exactly how you'd react. You played right in his hands and so did I."

"So what's to be done?" Lars asked.

"Nothing that bodes too well for you and me," she said grimly. "Or for your people and mine." She caught Lars' expression and shook her head. "God's Witness, I'm not giving up. I hope you don't think that!"

Lars gave her a half smile. "No, I don't suppose I do."

"Our lack of trust in one another played in his hands, Lars Haggart. Your—*dramatic* little exit this morning convinced the Board the Unborn are truly mad. Jeffrey couldn't have done better if he'd planned it himself. Still, something good's come out of the bad. He's forced you and me to work together—I don't think *that's* what he wanted."

"Damn it all," snapped Lars, "if what you say is true, I've got to ask *why*? What does Jeffrey hope to gain by all this deadly scheming? If my folk die in battle—"

Sister-Major stopped him with a look. She leaned forward intently, her eyes almost lost beneath her brows. "All I've told you, Lars Haggart, must never reach the ears of any other—even those you trust the most. And what I'm about to tell you now . . . Captain, there is a certain religious work that is as old as Mother Church. In the beginning, it was a part of The Book itself, but it was expunged from Holy Writ over a thousand years ago. It is *not* the inspired word of God, but the work of Satan himself. It's purpose is to snare the weak and unwary." Unconsciously, Sister-Major made The Sign on the table, in the moisture from her cup. "This book is the *Book of Armageddon*. It tells of the last, final battle between God and the Dark Adversary. I—I have every reason to believe Brother Jeffrey is a secret follower of that book."

Sister-Major paused, and it seemed to Lars as if she half expected the skies to open up and mark her words with thunder.

"Uh, forgive my ignorance," said Lars, "but what if he is, Sister? I'm surely no Church scholar, but it seems to me that's the kind of battle we're facing."

Sister-Major stared, her face the color of ash. "God help us—you're in Satan's hands yourself!"

"Stop it, now, I'm nothing of the sort! I merely asked a simple question."

"I'm—I'm *damned* if it is," she said shakily. "Captain, the followers of the *Book of Armageddon* believe they can best serve God by bringing that battle *about*. The sooner it comes, the sooner God wins, brings an end to mortal life and establishes His Own Kingdom."

"Well, doesn't He?"

"Doesn't who do what?"

"God. Doesn't He win out in the end as the Book says?"

"Of course he does!" she snapped. "You're missing the point, Captain. God gave us the will to *fight* Satan, not go belly up and take his blade. To Jeffrey's way of thinking, all we need do is simply throw ourselves at the demons, shouting Hallelujahs. If God's to win the day, it just brings His victory about all the sooner." She stopped and granted Lars a sour smile. "See what a fine role your folk are destined to play in hastening God's Kingdom?"

Lars' mouth was suddenly dry. "Damn, the man's mad as an owl! How—how many you think he has with him?"

"I wish I knew the answer," she said gravely.

Lars gripped the edge of his bench. "If you know all this, then stop him. You can't simply—let him keep running about loose!"

"Stop him how? I've no proof at all of what I'm saying. And who can I talk *to*? Which Brothers and Sisters can I trust?"

"You don't have to trust a one," Lars said flatly. "Go to the Holy Mother and talk to her. You *know* she'll hear you out!"

Sister-Major looked down at her hands. "Now I'll tell you the rest, Captain, and you'll think it's *me* that's totally daft. The Virgin Mother's a saint, and being what she is, she's as fair as fair can be. And that means, bless her, she'll lend an open ear to any Brother or Sister who cares to bend it." Sister-Major looked meaningfully at Lars. "That includes Brother Jeffrey, of course."

Lars looked appalled. "God's Witness, he wouldn't try to sell this Armageddon business to her!"

"No, he wouldn't dare that. Unless I miss my guess, what he *is* trying to do is nearly as cunning. You'll recall it was Jeffrey who warned you *not* to accept an 'offer that would come your way'? Telling you that, of course, made it almost certain that you would."

"True, but—"

"As sure as sin, Lars Haggart, it was Jeffrey himself who put the idea to see you in Holy Mother's head."

"What!"

"Yes, and to name you to the War Board as well. You see what he's done, do you not? He's set his trap and snared us both. You're the man who went berserk in council—a demon in disguise as some are saying. And I'm the *incompetent* Sister who failed to see what a danger you are." Lars read the plain, naked anguish in her eyes. "God may forgive him for that, but He'll not forget the other. On my faith, Lars Haggart, I'm certain he intends to cast doubt on Holy Mother Herself. If such a deed is even in his thoughts, he's condemned his soul to the pit!"

Lars didn't dare meet her eyes, for he suddenly saw a truth that turned his blood to ice. Sister-Major was shrewd in many matters, but there was an innocence about her that blinded her to the rest of Jeffrey's plan. Priest he might be, but Jeffrey had the morals of a snake. He knew what Lars knew only too well: That both a saint and a girl becoming a woman dwelled in Mother Anne Marie.

Damn the bastard—he's tossed the girl to me like a morsel to a dog! A flood of shame and anger colored his face, and he hoped Sister-Major didn't see it.

TWELVE

Late in the afternoon, clouds the color of slate began to sweep the low hills to the west. Lightning scorched the earth, and thunder bellowed from one far horizon to the other. Ragged veils of rain brushed the ground, mixing new smells of water and dust. The long columns of soldiers marching north felt the first swift rush of cool air and quickened their pace, as if a step or two faster would keep them dry. They knew, though, this was more than a summer rain. It was a storm that would soak them through, drag at their boots and mire their wagons in the mud. They'd shiver in sodden clothes all the night, and fight and die wet in the morning.

"It's God's blessing, is what it is," an old sergeant bawled at his men. "The demons are cursed with poor stubby legs, and they'll sink quicker'n you!"

It was close to ten when Lars wrapped his cloak tightly about him and made his way up the ridge. The rain had slowed to a drizzle, veiling the hard iron shapes of armor and sword. She saw him coming, and left the cluster of officers gathered about.

"Praise God, Lars Haggart. It's a foul night for certain."

"Demon weather," said Lars, "made to order for imps."

"Bite your tongue, Captain." Sister-Major made a face. "It's all I've been hearing since noon. Signs and omens and devil-eyes shining in the night. Word's spreading now they eat mud—that they draw their strength from it like God-fearing men from good bread."

And who feeds their fears with such drivel but the Church? thought Lars. *You've no one to blame but yourself. . . .*

"You'll go ahead, then, even if the weather doesn't clear?"

"The Book's ordained a battle," she said firmly. "A battle is what we'll have."

"If the demons decide to fight. . . ."

"Oh, they'll come out. They nearly always do."

Lars looked past her, at the watchfires glowing through the mist. The fires marked the farthest point of the lines; the dark earth beyond belonged to neither demon nor Mother Church. Wood was so scarce that all they had was what they'd brought, covered in wagons from the town. The five-thousand troopers gathered below would do without, facing the rain and wet as best they could.

"The Mazefield will suffer the most," said Sister-Major. "The leather and line won't trigger when they should. That's not going to help."

"That's one of the things I came to talk about," said Lars.

Sister-Major nodded. "More Churcher folk will die if the snares don't work, but your people will have a better chance."

"Maybe," Lars considered her words. "The demons know the weather will foul the maze. They'll be set on taking it with ease."

"—Which they will," Sister-Major added grimly. "Take whatever blessing God gives, Lars Haggart."

"Oh, I'll surely do that. . . ."

She caught the tone of his voice and raised her eyes. "You don't trust me, do you? God's Witness, I put my life in your hands with what I've shared!"

"And I'm putting mine in yours. And two hundred others besides."

"Your folk are in your own hands, Captain. That's the bargain we made."

"And it's a bargain you'll keep, will you not?"

Even in the dark, he saw her eyes grow hard. "Be at your post at first light," she said sharply. "See that your people are ready to fight." Turning swiftly away, she marched off and left Lars standing. He watched her disappear, then found his way back to camp.

In truth, he trusted the woman more than she imagined. It wasn't hard to guess how much her appalling revelations must have cost her. —Though she'd had little choice in the matter, he knew. Brother Jeffrey had her in a corner. She needed Lars desperately, as much as he needed her. More, most likely. If she'd picked him for an ally, she was truly at the end of her rope.

She'd get his loyalty and support, and he'd get command of his folk. The Karma Corps would *not* be spent in some suicidal charge, as Jeffrey hoped. That was the bargain they'd struck, and Lars had to admit she was as much at risk as he. If the War Board even guessed she was crossing their will. . . .

She could still betray him, he knew—say that he'd rebelled, refused to carry out her orders.

Damn it all, I've got to trust you, he said to himself. *If you turn against me, old woman, I swear I'll live through the fray and slit your throat. You've my Holy Oath on that. . . !*

Lars put a hollow laugh to his thoughts. That was the bloody catch, of course. Coming out alive. . . .

Lars had built a shelter against the rain. It was a cloth coated with wax, held down on one end with stones and propped up with sticks on the other. Carilee was waiting inside, arms wrapped tightly about her legs.

"I got blessed cold," she said solemnly. "Is it all right if I stay?"

"You know it is," he told her. "It's you angry with me, not the other way around."

"That hasn't changed, Lars. I came to get warm and nothing more."

"All right. Getting warm it is."

"You were talkin' to Sister-Major?"

"Up on the ridge just now."

She rubbed her hair dry as best she could and leaned against him. She trembled from the rain and he wrapped his heavy cloak about them both.

"The folk are talking, you know."

"I'd imagine they are," he said. "Just what are they talking about?"

"What's going to happen in the morning. Whether we'll make it or not."

"Aye, it's on my mind as well."

"And what do you think, Lars?"

He turned so he could see her. "What I *have* to think, Carilee. Whether I like it or not. That some will die and some won't."

Carilee trembled. "That's kind of—cold and cut and dried, is it not?"

"Of course it is," he said bluntly. "You asked what I thought, O'Farr. You already know how I *feel*, and that's something else indeed."

"I'm—I'm sorry," she said quickly, coming close against him. "I'm just scared, I guess. I think I wanted to hear something else."

"I know. And I wish there was something else to say."

Carilee was silent. Droplets of water raced in a line above her head, met at the edge of the shelter and ran down the pole like a vein.

"If we stay in these wet clothes all night, we'll be too sick to fight," said Lars.

"Good. Then let's do that. I'll pass the word to the others."

Lars grinned. "Our clothes won't get any drier if we wear 'em or take them off. But we will, for sure. And my cloak's big enough for us both."

"That's true, it is. I guess it'd be the healthy thing to do."

"Indeed it would, O'Farr."

"But just to keep warm and dry. Nothing else, Lars."

"Nothing else, of course."

"Don't make light of me," she warned. "I'm—I'm here to get warm and that's *all*. I've—no intention of giving in to your savage needs."

"You're a woman of good sense and reason," he said soberly. "I've always admired you for that. . . ."

Lars was up well before the dawn, clothed in clammy garments that felt like ice against his skin. He left Carilee and made his way down the hill.

Stars were showing through ragged tatters of cloud. At least, the sun would come up clear, and there'd be no fighting in the rain. Praise God for small favors.

As early as he was, his lieutenants were there before him. Lars joined them for cold mush and bread, deciding he'd best put something in his stomach. Amian Morse was there, and Eric and Sean and Maureen. Each commanded a troop of roughly fifty—two armed with crossbow and lance, and one with pike and axe. Sean's was the only troop proficient with the sword.

"We've been over this before," said Lars, "let's look at it once again." He scraped a spot in the dirt as they gathered around. "The Mazefield's a ruin after the rain, I don't have to tell you that. The trigger lines are wet, and when the full sun hits 'em they'll go off early or not at all. You can bet the imps won't give the engineers an extra minute to dry them out."

"So the demons will run right over the troops," Sean added. "They might not even need their jumpers, Captain."

"Oh, they'll be there," Lars corrected. "But they'll use them as sparingly as they can. Praise God they don't have more than they do." He raised his eyes to take in the others. "Sean's nearly right in what he says. They won't be using as many jumpers if the traps are weak. They never risk what they don't *have* to risk, and they've fought in bad weather before."

Amian Morse grunted. "Which means we'll maybe give them a little surprise."

"There's no reason we can't," said Lars. "We've never fought 'em before, and they won't be expecting to see us. It's an advantage we'll get but once, and we'd by God better make the most of it." Once more, he searched their faces. "There's no need not to say it, it's what we're all thinking. They're better and faster and they know how to fight. We've got to hit 'em and get out fast." He tapped the map in the dirt. "You'll get my sign when the jumpers are past the maze. I *don't* want to hit them inside—they're too fast and too practiced at that. When they break through we jump. Troop One to the left flank, Two to the right. Jump, loose your bolts and get out. Three and Four in reserve past the hill. And Sean, Amian—" He looked the two in the eye. "Don't fail to jump the reserves to new positions every two or three seconds."

"Sorry," growled Morse, "I never saw the purpose in all this shiftin' about, if we're not getting into the fight."

Lars shot him a look. "All the action *won't* be out there, lieutenant. Maybe you've forgotten what happened last time we got near a battle. We're bound to get some longjumpers, past the range of the others."

Amian flushed and looked at his boots. Lars had told him the truth, or part of it, at least. The rest was that Good Brother Jeffrey would have his eyes on them for sure—which meant Lars *had* to make it appear every trooper in the Corps was in the fight. Sister-Major had insisted on that, and Lars had readily agreed. With One and Two in the fray, and the reserves blinking in and out of sight, Jeffrey'd have a time telling who was doing what.

Young Sean cleared his throat. "You, uh—care to make a guess how many longjumpers we'll see, Captain?"

The boy knew very well Lars didn't, but had to ask. "Not as many as they'd like." Lars grinned. "If all the jumpers were longjumpers, Sean, they'd be dancing in Citadel this minute, and we'd be turning on spits." The others laughed, and Lars went on. "That's the only way I can answer your question. I hope to God there's not many. I'm certain there'll be more than we'd care to see. Get on back to your troops, now. I'll join you in a while."

The others wandered off, but Amian lagged behind. "All right if we talk?" he asked. "I won't keep you long."

"Make it quick," Lars said irritably. "I haven't got the time."

"I don't guess I ought to say it, but I will," Morse grumbled. "I'm ready to take some demon hides, Lars but I'd a lot rather we'd stood our ground at the barracks. Captain, we could have by God taken those Churchers!"

Lars stared. "Amian, what in hell are you saying?"

"Well we could, damn it. I don't like seeing you give in to that bitch."

"And how do you know I did?"

"We're here, aren't we?"

"You knew we'd have to fight some time. There wasn't much question of that. I did the best I could for us, Morse."

"Oh, now I'm not questioning that," Amian said without conviction.

Lars glanced up at the growing light. "Morse, did you ever wonder why the Churchers bring us fresh food and water every day. Not every week or so, but every *day?*"

"Huh?" Amian looked puzzled. "What's that got to do with anything?"

"Well it *could* have something to do with starving,"

Lars said flatly. He set his teeth and glared at Amian's belly. "Don't talk to me about making heroic stands, you fat bastard. By God, you'd be the first in the lot to surrender!"

THIRTEEN

The terrain was slightly different, the hills steeper and more pronounced than those at Essau Settlement to the west. Other than that, Lars would have sworn it was the same battleground as before. The Churchers took to the field, pikemen to the front and archers to the rear. Somewhere in the hills, the demon army gathered. When they were ready they'd come out howling, and hit the Churcher lines head on.

Not for the first time, Lars Haggart wondered how the war would have gone if there'd been no jumpers in the fray. The demons had forced the Churchers on the defensive right from the start, pressing them year after year into an ever-shrinking circle. It was a war Mother Church had to lose, for there was scarcely land left to raise crops to feed soldiers, and send them off to die. . . .

Lars looked up as a demon horn sounded, and the first smudge of dawn streaked the sky.

"The imps are up and about," Carilee sighed.

"So they are," said Lars.

"You ever wonder about 'em?"

"What, demons? Well of course I have. Everyone wonders about demons."

"I mean, what they're like, really. When they're not fighting and killing. What do they do? What do they eat? Where do they come from, Lars?"

Lars had to grin at the thought that popped into his head. "I don't know, I don't suppose they sit around drinking ale and telling tales. Doesn't ring right, does it?"

"The priests say they come from a fiery pit every morning, and hop back in it at night." Carilee made a face. "I don't believe that, do you?"

"Not greatly, no. Were you warm last night, I hope?"

"Quite warm, thank you."

"Good. I wouldn't have you catching a cold."

"Lars. I *don't* wish to talk about last night. Not any at all."

"All right then, we won't."

"I guess you're proud of yourself, aren't you? Tricking me like that."

"Ah, that's what it was, then." Lars nodded in understanding. "Trickery and such."

"You know very well it was. At least," she muttered to herself, "all of you was there. You weren't off somewhere else."

"Carilee—"

"No, *don't*." She warned him with a look. "I think last night was a mistake. I'm still angry, Lars, I'm sorry. Something's not right and—well, I don't much like what it is."

"Everything seemed right enough to me."

"Well it wasn't. Not right at all."

"You're imagining things, O'Farr. Can't you see that plain?"

"Oh, no I'm not," she said with a bitter little laugh. "*She's* still there, all right. . . ."

"For God's sake, Carilee! I never even—" He stopped then, and stood up straight. The grating wail of demon horns saved him from a lie. The muddy hills wavered, and sprouted an ugly crop. A terrible din rent the air as impish legions struck their shields. For a long moment, the awful sound deafened every ear. Then, upon some silent signal, blood-red pennons stabbed the air and the demons charged.

"Stay close to me," Lars said tightly, pulling Carilee to him.

Carilee nodded, tossed Lars a crossbow from the ground, and gripped another herself. The demons swarmed down from the hill. Churcher sergeants flung up their fists, and pikemen braced their weapons to meet the foe.

"Steady . . . steady. . . ." Lars muttered, and glanced over his shoulder. His troops were well placed, hidden between the slopes of two hills where their scouts could see the battle. There'd be no blind jumping today; the bowmen would have to see their marks and hit them well.

The armies met like thunder, but Lars paid the battle little heed. His eyes were locked beyond the killing ground, far to the army's rear. They were there, somewhere. He couldn't see them but he could feel them, sense their deadly presence.

Suddenly, the left wing of the Churchers gave a roar and surged ahead. The demon lines buckled, fell back and ran. Battle horns squealed and reinforcements poured down from the hills. Fresh troopers threw themselves in the right and filled the gap. The demon lines wavered, fell back again and held.

And then Lars saw them, padding in silent ranks behind a wedge of demon warriors. His skin crawled at the sight, though they looked no different from the rest. They waited, huddled close together, dark fur eating up the light.

"There," he pointed, his voice almost a whisper. "Just past the double flag."

"I see them," said Carilee. "Oh Lord, there's so—*many* of 'em!"

Two-hundred, perhaps, Lars guessed. Somewhat more than half of what they had. *And now they've the longjumpers, too. How many of those devils do we face?*

"Lars, look." Carilee gripped his arm and pointed. Lars saw it at once. Bloody pennons dipped along the front, and the demons charged again. They'd found a weakness in the lines, and now they swarmed to take it with a will.

Lars held his breath. His heart beat frantically against his chest. If the demons broke through, it would happen in a moment. The jumpers would follow the wedge, take the ruined Mazefield and rip through the rear of the Churcher ranks. And a second before that he'd commit his troops to the battle. If they hit the demons just right. . . .

A familiar itch worried the back of his neck. Once more, his eyes swept the rear of the demon ranks. There was something. . . . something he knew he ought to see. Something that—

"Carilee!" Lars went rigid and gripped her arm until she winced. "Carilee, signal the leaders to me. Hurry!" She turned without asking the reason and gave the sign. At once, Lars' four lieutenants popped into sight before him.

"Listen, and listen well," Lars said tightly. "Eric, Maureen—in a moment, the regulars will start their final charge and back the Churchers against the maze. When they do, the jumpers'll make their move." He paused, and a grin stretched the corners of his mouth. "Only we won't wait for that. We won't hit 'em at the Mazefield at all. We'll stop them *behind* their own lines, hit them before they're ready to fight!"

The four started talking at once. Lars held up a hand to stop them. "It's the only advantage we've got. We'll get in, hit 'em, and get out fast. One and Two—lose your bolts and jump back. We'll only get one chance to catch them by surprise. With luck, though, we'll knock a hell of a lot of them out."

Lars paused, and let his gaze take in Sean and Morse. "Eric, you and Maureen will jump *back* to the top of the hill, just above your launching point. If there are longjumpers about, they'll see you for sure. Don't *stay* there more'n a second. Jump again and get the hell out. Go all the way back to Citadel before you stop. I don't want you near this place with empty weapons."

Understanding suddenly dawned on Amian's face. "And that's what we're for, then. My troops and Sean's."

"Right. The longjumpers will be expecting crossbowmen who can't fight back. You'll be here instead—a hundred men with swords and axes and pikes."

"It sounds good," said Maureen, "damned if it doesn't, Lars."

"It'll work," Eric nodded. "I like it a lot better than the other."

"It'll work if we do it right," said Lars. "Get back and send me a scout from each troop. Go on, we haven't time to dawdle!" The officers disappeared. Instantly, the four scouts appeared in their place. Lars pointed out the horde of jumpers and the scouts stepped back.

Lars watched, one fist grinding intently against another. *Wait . . wait. . . .* It had to be just right . . . not a moment too soon or a moment after. . . .

There! Suddenly, the jumpers came together, hefting their axes in their fists. *Closer you bastards, come on!* Lars picked a spot on the flank of the hill, not thirty meters above the demon horde. "*Now,*" he shouted to the scouts, "bring them in on me!" Raising one arm high, he gripped the crossbow and vanished. Abruptly, he stood on the slope above the foe. A hundred crossbowmen landed at his side, loosing their bolts at once in the midst of demon jumpers. The attack took them completely by surprise. Massed together as they were, the imps could scarce avoid the hail of deadly missiles. In that hairthin breath of a moment before it happened, Lars could see it all in his mind's eye—furred warriors screaming as the bolts tore through their flesh, falling away like wheat before a scythe. "*We've done it,*" he shouted aloud. "*We've broken the bastards' backs!*"

Only it didn't happen at all. . . .

The demons were there and then they weren't. Bolts cleaved air and hit nothing. Lars knew it couldn't happen but it did. In one awful moment of understanding he knew the truth, but there was no time at all to take it back. In half the blink of an eye, his troopers spent their bolts and vanished to the safety of the hill behind the battle—

—and found the longjumpers waiting there to meet them.

In less than half a minute it was over, but Lars Haggart lived every second as if it were a thousand years. There was precious little time to jump again, for the demons were in their midst, hacking grimly away with murderous axe and blade. It was butchery quick as a wink, the dying already dead before they fell. A few of Lars' people found their wits and disappeared, but only a few. Some brought empty crossbows up to bear, frantically squeezing triggers as red-eyed demons took their lives.

The slaughter had scarce begun before Amian Morse and Sean brought their troops into the fray. They jumped in the thick of the fight, sun-silver flashing off their blades. Lars shouted a warning as the imps turned to shadow—vanished and reappeared directly behind the attacking force. One man screamed and then another as the demons took their toll. Soldiers whirled about to meet the foe and found him gone. Amian Morse bellowed like a bull, slashing his blade in anger at empty air. When he saw the dead around him, he stumbled back in horror. Suddenly, howls from his left brought him around. Lars saw them too. The longjumpers waited, not thirty meters away, raising iron weapons in a challenge. Amian's face went dark. He shook his sword in answer, and shouted to his men.

"No, Amian, don't!" Lars sprinted toward his friend, knowing he was already too late. Amian and his soldiers disappeared, Sean's men directly on his heels.

Cursing under his breath, Lars jumped into the fight. A demon met him face to face, red saucer eyes full of hate. An axe found the edge of Lars' blade, numbing his arm to the shoulder. Lars staggered back, slashed out wildly and saw his weapon hit home. The longjumper howled, dropped his axe and grappled his belly. Lars came in for the kill as the demon vanished. Carilee screamed a warning and Lars ducked. Iron hummed wickedly close to his head. Lars stepped back, felt white heat sear his flesh and went down. The second demon was on him with a vengeance, slashing and cutting at the ground. Lars doubled in pain and vanished, then jumped twice again for good measure.

Shaking his head he came to his knees. He was somewhere down the hill, close to the rear of the maze. He could hear the din of battle to his left. Gritting his teeth, he brought one leg up under the other. Bile came to his throat and he fell to the ground and retched.

"You all right, Cap'n?"

"Huh, what?" Lars blinked, and saw the Churcher soldier at his side. "Yes, I—guess so." He started to rise and fell back. The soldier caught him and helped him stand. "Got to—got to get back," Lars said weakly. He tried to jump, but nausea brought him down. The soldier helped him to his knees. A water jar appeared at Lars' face. He took it in his hands and brought it shakily to his lips. "Thanks," he muttered. "I'm grateful, friend. . . ."

For the first time, he turned and looked at the Churcher. He was a wiry, leather-faced trooper with tiny dark eyes and features like a rat. He grinned at Lars and showed prominent yellow teeth.

"I'm Ham, Joshua's son, from Davidtown." He looked curiously at Lars. "Never seen any of you Unborn up close. Why, yer looks near human, you do."

Lars sucked in a breath. "Look, I've got to—get to my folk. You think you could—" His words were cut short as two blunt explosions sounded in their midst. The Churcher went white as Carilee and young Kurt appeared. He dropped his water jar and ran.

"God's Breath," Carilee cried, taking him in her arms, "I thought you were dead for certain!"

Lars didn't answer. He tried to move but she held him, tears streaking the dirt on her cheeks. "Wait, Lars, you're hurt. Let Kurt put a cloth 'round your leg to stop the blood. . . ."

"Just leave me alone, Carilee. . . ."

"Lars, you mustn't—"

"Leave me alone, damn you!" His arm came up like a log, struck her solidly in the face and sent her sprawling. Carilee cried out, and stared in disbelief. Lars stumbled to his feet, tore off his belt and wrapped it tightly about his thigh. Without looking back, he staggard drunkenly up the hill. The pain seared his leg like a brand. Lars ground his teeth, drank in the pain like wine and prayed for more.

All the way up the slope he met his dead. They were sprawled in twos and threes, where Sean and Amian Morse had followed the demons' dare. When he reached the killing ground atop the hill he saw the rest, frozen still in tangled contortions of death. He made his way through the carnage as if he saw them clear, and yet saw nothing at all. *God, no, so many . . . it can't be as many as this . . . !*

Someone called his name.

Lars didn't stop.

He found Amian's broad, naked back and the sight suddenly filled him with terrible anger. Blood blinded his eyes and he jerked Morse around, drew back his fists and pounded him savagely in the face.

"Goddamn fool," he cursed, "you killed them all, you simple bastard! You led them up—the—hill— and killed them all!"

He punctuated his words with one slashing blow after another. Amian didn't move. He stared past Lars, letting Lars' hands turn him to meat.

When they finally pulled him off, Lars saw the girl

for the first time. She lay at Amian's feet, a small and slender maid with cornflower hair and no face at all. Lars tried to jerk free but the troopers held him firm. He screamed and called them names and spat in their faces. Finally, a soldier he didn't know shook his head in regret and hit him solidly in the jaw.

He sat alone on the hill and watched the Churchers search for their dead. He knew her steps and didn't have to turn.

"Did you win or lose or can you tell?" he said dully.

"Won, I guess," said Sister-Major. "Winning's when they don't break through. I'm sorry, Lars Haggart. I saw some of the fight, and guess I know the rest."

"Oh, do you now?" Lars said bluntly. "Then explain it to me, Sister." When she didn't answer, he turned. There was a patch of dried blood above one eye. Her helmet was gone, and a piece of leather armor hung from her chest. "I brought two hundred up and jumped a hundred over there. We loosed our bolts and missed. That—that couldn't happen, but it did. The demons followed us back, and killed sixty of those. My reserves chased the devils up the hill—or so they imagined—and we lost another thirty. God's Witness, that's only ninety—less than half, right? Not overly bad for our first real battle. And it took no time at all—sixty, seventy seconds at the most."

"Captain Haggart, listen—"

"No, *you* listen," Lars snapped. His eyes met hers and blazed. "It's over. You can tell the War Board that. They'll be pleased enough, I think. We've spilled our blood for the Church!" He threw back his head and gave her a terrible grin. "You brought us to life for no reason, Sister-Major. Even the fools at Citadel should have the sense to see it now."

"Captain," she said almost gently, "please believe I know how you feel. Even those in command are entitled to their grief."

"My God, I'm not in *command* of anything. Can't you get that through your head?"

"Look you, Lars Haggart," she said firmly, a sudden edge to her voice. "I'm sorry for what happened. I can't bring them back. And *don't* vent your anger on me, young man—it was *you* spent them all, not me. By the Sign, man, what *happened*? Can you doff your martyr's robe long enough to tell me that!"

Lars clenched his fists. "It—came to me when I saw it. They were bunched up fine behind the lines. I saw—I saw no sense in committing them to the maze. I wanted to catch the devils unaware. . . ."

Sister-Major nodded. "I didn't say the plan was wrong. I asked you why it failed."

Lars looked up, somewhat surprised by her words. "They beat us," he said plainly. "It's as simple as that. They're better and they're faster. I told you that from the start."

"Yes, you did, Lars Haggart. That's not what I'm talking about, and you know it."

Lars faced her, but said nothing.

"You saw something out there," she pressed him. "What was it, Captain?"

"I told you what I saw, damn it. You want to hear it again?"

Sister-Major turned away. "Hide it from me if you like. I don't think you can hide it from yourself. . . ."

FOURTEEN

Lars stomped about the loft, kicking hay aside and cursing to himself. He circled the narrow chamber a dozen times, then stopped and let his gaze sweep every corner.

"Nothing, not a bloody damn thing," he swore between his teeth. "You've drained them all dry, you have, every blessed—*aha!*" His face split in a grin as the fat clay pot caught his eye. "There you are, you bitch. Hidin' out, were you?" His fingers grasped the vessel, then his smile disappeared. He stared at the empty pot in disbelief, then swept back his arm and hurled it angrily against the wall.

"Damn and *blast* your soul!" he bellowed. The pot smashed in a thousand tiny pieces. Shards bounced off the wall and rattled about the room. Lars jammed his hands in his belt and flared out the window. "Bad ale, and not enough of it," he grumbled. "All a man can expect from the bloody Church."

He heard her climb the ladder, but pretended she wasn't there.

"Ah, me, it's only you," Carilee sighed. "I thought perhaps the pigs were havin' a fight."

"What pigs?" Lars Haggart muttered. "What the hell are you talkin' about?"

"Why, the pigs I can smell," she answered. "The ones you're clearly keeping in this sty of yours, Lars. . . ."

"I'm in no mood for your wit, Carilee."

"Wasn't meant to be wit at all, Captain Haggart."

"You don't like the smell, the ladder goes down as well as up."

Carilee watched him in silence. "You planning on staying up here forever? You'd feel some better if you'd get cleaned up and have some food. It's been three days now, Lars."

"Three, is it?" Lars was genuinely surprised. "I'd have said five or six."

"Lars—turn around and look at me, damn you!"

"All right. . . ." Lars turned, with no expression at all. "I'm looking. What is it you want, O'Farr?"

"I—I want you to get some sense in your head, for a start."

"Why? What for? What's the good of that?"

"My *God*. . . ." Carilee shook her head in disgust. "I never thought to see you like this."

Lars glared and ground his teeth. "You must have come up here for something. What the hell was it?"

"Would you like to hear the news? Does the subject interest you at all?"

"No," he said flatly, "it doesn't."

Carilee held his eyes. "The fighting's going something fierce. The demons are hitting two sides of the front at a time. They've *never* done that before. Sister-Major says—"

Lars looked up sharply. "She's been here? You've been talking to her?"

Carilee let out a breath. "She's been here *four* times, Lars. I've told you all this before."

"Yes, well I'm afraid I don't recall."

"It's the first time you've been half sober when I said it."

"More's the pity for that. What else did she have to say?"

"That the jumpers *learned* something after the last battle. That it's likely 'cause of them the demons are pushing all the harder." Carilee paused, and gave him a curious look. "Sister-Major says you'd know more about that. What does she mean, Lars? Do you? *Is* there something you know?"

"Damned woman's crazy as an owl," Lars muttered. He turned quickly away, before she could read his eyes.

"Is she? Well at least she's not brooding in a loft, and—"

"Carilee, *stop* it, will you?" He turned to face her again, and this time it was hard to meet her eyes. "Look, are you—all right, O'Farr? Honest to God, I never meant to strike you. I wasn't thinking straight, I just—lashed out at whoever was there."

"I know," she said gently. "I know you didn't mean it."

"Well—I'm sorry. You know that, don't you?"

"Yes, Lars, I do."

"How is—how's Amian? Is he all right?"

"I guess you'd say he is."

"Tell him I'm sorry, Carilee. I shouldn't have done that, and God's Witness, I didn't know the girl was dead. Damn it all, he must know I wasn't myself."

"No, Lars. . . ."

"What?"

Carilee's eyes turned to ice. "I will not make your

apologies for you, Lars Haggart. God, look at you. You're not even man enough now to do that!"

Lars went rigid. Carilee felt his rage brush her mind. The power of the fury locked inside him scared her badly but she refused to back away. "Oh, there's one thing more," she said evenly. "The Virgin Mother's summoned you twice." She gave him a honey-sweet smile. "Says it's *most* urgent that she see you."

"Get out of here, Carilee. . . ."

Sergeant O'Farr raised her near-perfect nose and sniffed in his direction. "I wouldn't *dream* of stayin', Captain Haggart . . ."

"A pretty maid's a fine fair thing,
but maids grow old and dry—aye . . .
Ale, me boy, is the thing to wed,
for it lasts until you diii—aye . . ."

Lars laughed, held the pot over his face and let it fill his mouth. Half the liquid ran down his shirt, and made him laugh all the more. Holding the pot by the neck, he stumbled out of the barracks, paused, and took a second swallow. He'd remembered, finally, where he'd hidden the pot three days before, after he'd gathered every jar and jug he could carry and taken them to the loft.

The summer night blazed with stars. Lars wondered if there were really that many, or if his ale had doubled the number.

"Pretty . . . ver' pretty," he mumbled. "Wish to hell I was—out there somewhere, 'stead of where I am."

Past the palisade walls, pale points of gold winked in the town. Citadel tower was etched against the dark, but if any lights were there, Lars couldn't see them.

"What I—what I oughta do is hop up an' see that pretty lass . . . see 'f she wants a touch of ale." Taking another cautious sip, he held the jug up and shook it. It was still a quarter full, but that wouldn't last. He thought about that, his mind trying desperately to grasp the dilemma at hand. There wasn't another drop in the barracks, he was near certain of that.

Lars stopped in his tracks and frowned. If a man wanted ale, where would he go to get it? The answer came almost at once, and he laughed aloud. *Taverns,* by God! Why, that's what taverns were for. They had all the ale in the world—kegs, barrels and tubs of the stuff. A man could take a bath in ale if he liked!

A sudden picture flashed in his head. He and Anne Marie were in an enormous vat of ale. Lars was drinking as fast as he could. When he emptied the vat he could see her, a sleek little pretty clothed in froth. The thought was too awesome to imagine, and he shook his head in wonder.

Lurching to the palisade door, he stopped and considered the problem. Drunk as a lord he might be, but he hadn't lost his wits. Karma Corps troopers didn't walk about the town in the black of night. Not 'less they wanted a cracked head in the morning, or worse than that. Lars leaned against the gate and drained the last dregs of his pot. If he couldn't walk about and find a tavern . . . A foolish grin slid off his face. God's Breath, of course! Just *think* about a warm and friendly tavern, good folks sittin' abou—

Lars yelled and churned his legs in midair. He hit the first awning, ripped through it cleanly and kept going. The second slowed him down, but not enough to help. A stack of wooden crates filled the alley, and Lars hit them dead center. The crates exploded into kindling and Lars plowed through them with great speed.

For a moment he lay quite still, frightened out of his wits. He knew exactly what he'd done. It was a simple, but potentially deadly error. He'd never *been* in a Churcher tavern. Therefore, he had no idea where one could be found. No doubt, he'd been in a tavern in some past life. Likely more than one. Why, then, had he picked one to remember a good two stories off the ground?

Grumbling to himself, he stood and brushed splinters off his clothes. A window clattered open. A shrill voice cursed his manner of birthing, and his mother's relations with swine. Verbal abuse was followed by a barrage of greater substance. Lars leaped aside as old vegetables and other matter came his way.

The cobbled streets twisted up the hill, in no apparent order. Soon, Lars found himself exactly where he'd been the moment before. Finally, the flickering oil lamp caught his eye and he set his course for it, as straight as his legs would allow. A carved wooden sign read THE CELIBATE MONK'S INN. Lars grinned and stumbled over the sill. A thick tallow candle was the only light in the room. There were four keg tables circled with burly Churcher warriors. At Lars Haggart's appearance, they looked up as a man, blinked in disbelief and made the Sign. Lars gave them a friendly nod and gripped the bar.

"Ale, if you please," he said politely. "In the largest tankard you have."

The innkeeper was squat and dark and ugly. His eyes were drops of oil, and they clearly didn't care for what they saw. Still, the coins Lars had tossed upon his counter were real enough. With a glance over his shoulder, he passed the problem quickly to the others.

The ale was dark and smelled of honey, and went down Lars Haggart's gullet with great ease. Lars sighed and wiped foam off his lips. "Another like that," he told the keeper. "It's for certain the finest ale I've ever had!"

"—And the last you'll be drinkin' in here. . . ."

Lars looked to his left and saw the heavy set guardsman at his side. Turning to his right he found another, a perfect match for the first.

"Well, then," he grinned, "if you don't like it here, why don't we all go somewhere else?"

The soldier didn't smile. Instead, he jerked Lars around with his big right hand and brought his left up fast in a killing punch. Lars ducked, felt the fist brush his skull and kneed the Churcher in the crotch. The man groaned and clutched his vitals. His friend brought a tankard down solidly on the back of Lars' head. Lars dropped to the floor, stars dancing wildly before his eyes. A big boot came down hard to crack his fingers. Lars jerked his hand away in time, wrapped his arm tightly about a leg and tried desperately to clear his head. The fellow cursed and tossed him free. Lars rolled to the wall, picked himself up and staggered to his feet. The soldier came at him in a crouch. Lars grabbed a chair and held it before him like a shield. The man hesitated an instant too long— Lars whipped the chair over his shoulder and brought it down hard. The chair splintered with a satisfying sound; Lars' foe dropped like an ox. Lars grinned, looked up and saw what was coming. The grin faded fast and Lars scrambled for the door.

The Churcher warriors were on him like a plague. They swarmed out of their chairs, tossing mugs aside and whooping with delight. A boot found his rear and sent him reeling. Lars grabbed for the wall as a big fist hit him in the belly. Another pounded his head like a hammer. Something found his leg and started methodically twisting it off.

In a still coherent corner of his mind, Lars wondered if he'd smother before they beat him to death. As he pondered this question, he noted something peculiar taking place. Instead of getting bigger, the heap was rapidly shrinking in size. Boots were disappearing, meaty fists and ugly faces falling away. Lars wondered if God had decided to run life backwards.

A vaguely familiar face looked down at him and grinned, reached out for his hand and hauled him to his feet.

"Don't remember me, do you? We talked after the battle, we did."

Suddenly, the pit-black eyes and rodent beak fell in place. "By damn, yes," said Lars. "Ham, Joshua's son from Davidtown, right?"

The little man looked pleased. "That's me, for sure." He spat on his hands and rubbed them down his jacket. "If yer through passin' time with these lads, might be a fair idea if we took our leave. You any objection to that?"

Lars ran a hand over his jaw and winced. Past Ham's shoulder, the men who'd pummeled him to the floor had grudgingly returned to their ale. One still lay on his back blowing air. Another held a rag to his bloody face. "I'd say it's a fair idea," Lars agreed. "The service here's fine, but the entertainment's not to my liking."

Ham laughed, showed Lars a feral set of teeth and

ushered him out. The night had cooled some, and the fresh air brought Lars to his senses.

"You mind greatly if I pose a question?" he asked the other. "You're not a man of great size—no offense—yet you pulled that bunch of bears off me easy as sin. I'd be curious to hear just how."

Ham twitched his nose. "Some is big and some's quick, some's smart and some ain't. Me, I'm smart and quick both. And a master of dirty tricks besides." His bright eyes sparked up at Lars. "You mind *me* askin' one? What led you to leave your own and venture here, for God's sake?"

"Sheer stupidity," sighed Lars. "And besides, I ran out of drink."

Ham threw back his head and laughed, a curious sound like rapid little coughs. "By the Holy Hand itself, yer lucky ol' Ham found you. Good ale I've got, and somethin' far better than that!"

Lars wondered what had happened to his tongue. The best he could figure was that it had suddenly turned to stone. —Along with his legs, an arm and various bodily parts.

"God's Breath," he said, struggling to get out the words, "wha—whazoo—what in alla *hells* am I drinking?"

Ham's ferret nose and inky eyes swam into focus. He leaned toward Lars and spoke in a whisper. "Better'n any ale, now ain't it? Make it outa *corn*, is what I do."

Lras blinked. "Corn?"

"Aye, corn. Never heard of corn ale, did you?" He shared a sly wink with Lars. "Won't, either, 'less you're drinkin' with Ham."

"Lord God," breathed Lars, trying to shake the

webs out of his head. "I never trank, uh—drank, anything like it." He squinted at the wondrous liquid in his cup. It was plain and clear as water, but water it surely was not. It burned going down, then throbbed like a coal in a man's belly. After a moment, it sent out tiny fires to turn the body to stone. Lars had no idea how many cups he'd had. Or how long he'd been in his new companion's quarters. Or where, God's Mercy, those quarters might be.

"You're a fine fellow," he told Ham. "Don't care if y'are a bloody Churcher."

Ham laughed. As far as Lars could recall, he'd laughed at everything either of them had said. "And you ain't bad yourself. For a—a devil-spawned son of the Unborn."

Lars spilled ale down his front. It was clearly the funniest thing he'd ever heard. When he could find his wits again, he pointed a shaky finger at Ham. "You know wh-what you are? Huh? Huh? You're a—sawed-off son of a celibate priest."

"If I am, then you're a—a f-fur-bellied demon's rear end!"

"And you're a f-f-fat-assed Sister's big toe."

"You've got a face like p-pig droppings flattened under a wagon!"

"And you've got a nose like a—"

Of a sudden, Ham's dark eyes went wide. He sat up straight and looked wildly over his shoulder down the stairs. "G-God's Breath, friend Lars, it's *her!* You've got t-to get out of here fast!"

Lars blinked. "Her? Who's her?"

"My *wife*," Ham whined, pushing Lars away from the table to a corner of the room. "If she catches us up here drinking she'll k-kill me sure!"

"Get out where?" Lars asked. "Damn it all, Ham—"

"Out the window, quick," Ham moaned. "Do it, Lars, hurry!"

Lars peered out the small window. He wasn't too drunk to note it was a good three stories off the ground.

"Ham Joshua's son, who've you got up there," a voice shrieked. "If it's corn drink I smell you're dead as dirt!"

Lars' mouth fell open. Looming at the top of the stairs was the largest woman he'd ever seen in his life. At once, the lady saw him as well and knew what he was. One of the feared Unborn was in her very own house, right before her eyes. Its shirt was damp and dark, no doubt with her poor husband's blood. The woman's face turned to ash. She threw her arms in the air and began to scream.

Ham tried desperately to climb the wall.

Lars jumped, an image of his own friendly loft in his head. . . .

Only the loft wasn't there. Or if it was, Lars wasn't in it. Instead, he was nowhere at all. No ground no sky no nothing. Only Lars Haggart himself, adrift in a no-color place that wasn't truly a place at all.

Lars shouted, but no sound met his ears.

Lars thrashed about, but there was no place to go.

Lars waited, having nothing else to do. In a moment, something appeared in the corner of his eye. A moment after that, it floated into view. Lars saw it at once, and knew who it was. It was John-William, who'd Drifted a few days before. John-William stared, clearly as surprised to see Lars as Lars was to see him.

FIFTEEN

God's Breath, Lars moaned to himself, *I'm bloody dead again!*

The thought passed as quickly as it had come. As logical as it seemed, he knew it wasn't so.

If that's true, then John-William isn't dead either. And that means both of us are somewhere else. . . .

Before he could ponder that, another figure appeared in John-William's wake. Lars recognized her at once. It was Elaine, young Sean's lover. He'd sat beside the lad and watched her Drift the year before. Elaine saw Lars and stretched her arms out to reach him. Lars tried to help, but his motions did nothing to bring them closer. Lars watched as some unseen current carried her off. As long as he could see her, she mouthed a single silent word: *Sean . . . Sean . . . Sean . . . !*

There were other Drifters about, but none close enough for him to see who they were. They floated like lonely motes in an endless room, never getting overly close or farther away.

For all the strangeness of his surroundings, Lars felt oddly at ease. He sensed, somehow, that nothing could happen to him here. Perhaps, he decided, because this was a place where nothing had ever happened and never would. He wasn't at all concerned that he'd share John-William's fate. It was something he simply knew. John-William couldn't escape, but he could. He wasn't a part of this, he was merely passing through.

Passing through to where, for God's sake!

There was another thing he knew that should have frightened him but didn't. John-William and the girl had only *seemed* to move close and then away. There was no such thing in this place as close and far—no moment between the time they'd seemed to be where they were and then gone. Lars knew for certain not the smallest part of a second had ever passed or ever would. He wasn't sure how he knew, he simply did.

Another thing that didn't exist was the aftereffect of drink. Lars had never been more sober in his life. Even the bilious taste of Ham's corn ale had disappeared. This was surely a double blessing, he decided. Clearly, drinking and jumping didn't mix. He wondered why no one had learned this before, and saw the answer at once: No one but Lars Haggart himself had been foolish enough to try.

Lars took another long look at the vast stretch of nothing. Wherever he was or wasn't, it was time to be somewhere else. This time, he was in no hurry at all. He let himself relax, took half a dozen long and easy breaths, and made absolutely certain his image was clear. Weathered wood and soft light, the sweet smell of hay and the shape of eaves coming together over his head.

Lars vanished—

—reappeared

—and fell drunkenly to the ground, retching between his hands. He shook all over as Ham's corn ale and everything else he'd ever consumed tried to exit his body at once. Cold sweat peppered his face. He gasped for breath and spit bile. *God's Holy Eyes, it has to stop soon . . . I've nothing left to give!*

His stomach, though, knew this wasn't so. The terrible nausea caught him up again and sent him reeling. Lars gave in and let the business run its course. It suddenly dawned on him what had happened. No time had passed since he'd left good Ham and his screaming spouse. Floating about with John-William had merely delayed what had to be.

Finally, Lars fell back exhausted and stared up at a cloudless sky. Plainly, he was not in the loft at all. Somehow, he'd missed the target again. He was outside the town, and it was morning. He hadn't imagined the night had passed so swiftly, but clearly it had. Sitting up, he stretched tight muscles and looked about. He was weak and empty, but he felt some better. There was a tall stand of trees to his left. Frost had touched the high top branches and turned the leaves a brilliant red. A bird saw Lars, squawked its displeasure and flapped away. At the base of the trees, dry grasses were—

Lars froze, a quick chill climbing the back of his neck. "Red Leaves, my father's nose," he said aloud. "It's the middle of bloody summer, not autumn!"

The shouts brought him about, and Lars saw them bounding over the hill, waving their weapons in the air. They were dressed in dark blue cloth and heavy mail, and brandished oaken shields embossed in bronze. A few wore leather helms, but most bared their heads to the morn; they were tall, stocky giants of men with pale blue eyes and flaxed beards. Yellow hair hung to their shoulders and danced in the wind.

Lars stared at the sight in open wonder. Whoever

they were, they weren't Churchers for sure. He'd
never seen them before, yet they somehow looked
terribly familiar.

Suddenly, the men stopped as one, and braced
heavy boots against the ground. A volley of spears
flashed through the sky. Lars looked up and watched
the display with interest. The spears came to earth
and quivered in the ground, none more than a meter
from where he stood. Startled, Lars came to his
senses and backed away. It hadn't occurred to him
before, but now it seemed perfectly clear. The bastards were after *him*—and not for the first time,
either. He couldn't say exactly where or when, but
these yellow-haired louts had tried to kill him more
than once.

A loud bellowing chorus shattered the quiet. With
an ominous ring of metal against metal, the warriors
drew heavy axes from their belts and charged down
the hill. Lars turned and ran for the nearby trees.
The woods were thick with second growth that tore
at his jerkin and trousers. He could hear the men
behind him, and knew they were gaining ground
fast. Pausing to catch his breath, he saw the forest
thinned a bit to his right. An ax-chewed wood beside
his head. Lars let out a cry and ran for his life. The
ground began to slope, adding to his speed. A small
creek appeared and he took it in his stride, scrambled up the bank and kept going. A few meters
farther, the forest ended abruptly. Lars' heart sank.
There was nothing but open meadow, as far as the
eye could see. He could outrun some of the madmen
on his trail, but certainly not the lot. Heavy boots
splashed water over his shoulder. Lars started his
legs churning and didn't look back.

Sweat stung his eyes and his lungs were near to

bursting. He cursed his rat-faced companion and all
the corn ale he'd ever made. The warriors behind
him were used to this sort of thing. Lars definitely
wasn't. In another few moments—

Something caught his eye to the left, moving quickly
toward him through high brown grass. Without slowing his pace, he watched the things approach, saw
them leave the grass and burst into open meadow.
Lars' skin crawled and he almost stopped in his
tracks. They were warriors, companions of those at
his back, but he hardly noted that at all. It was the
creatures they were *sitting* upon that struck him
cold. They were neither pigs nor oxen, but something leaner and far swifter; sleek-tendoned beasts
with powerful legs and heads like hammers. Like the
warriors themselves, these beasts were strangely
familiar. *God's Breath,* Lars thought of a sudden,
I've sat one of the damnable things myself! The image took him aback, but there was precious little
time to take it further. The riders were nearly upon
him, broadswords whirling in their fists, ready to cut
him into bait. Lars stumbled, came to his feet and
saw heavy thrashing hooves bearing down upon him.

Lars Haggart jumped.

The warriors and the meadow disappeared. *Damn
me for a fool, why didn't I think of that before!*
Looking about, he saw he was standing on the bank
of a lazy river. Trees with gracefully bowed branches
lined the shore. The tips of these branches trailed
long green leaves into the water. Lars heard sounds
and stopped to listen. It was laughter, and close at
hand, and with this pleasant hum and chatter came
the fine crackly smell of roasting meat.

Having experienced enough surprises for one day,
Lars approached the scene with great caution. Peer-

ing through a stand of heavy brush, he saw twenty or more cheery folk in the clearing. They were people of all ages, from babes barely crawling to gray-haired oldsters. All were dressed in brightly dyed wool and leather, a dozen shades of scarlet and blue, and green and butter and rust. Meat turned on a spit, and there were tables of fruits and breads and kegs of ale. Lars made a face at the latter, but could scarcely take his eyes off the food.

The place looked peaceful enough, and he decided to chance it. Parting the brush, he walked into the clearing across the green. Here and there, people glanced up and looked him over, but no one seemed alarmed. After a few short steps, two lovely girls stepped into his path. They stopped and faced him shyly, hands clasped demurely behind their backs.

"You're new hereabouts, are you not?" smiled the first. "I'd remember of a certain if I'd seen you before."

The other girl giggled behind her hand. One was yellow-haired, the other dark. Both were cheerful maids, with flesh of honey and cream—a great deal of which, Lars noted, peeked past the necks of their gowns to please the eye.

"I think I've been here before," Lars said honestly, "but certainly not of late."

"Well you *are* here now," the first said gaily, "and that's what counts, does it not!" Each took one of his hands and laughingly pulled him along. Lars grinned, and followed without complaint. The raven-haired girl offered him ale, which Lars politely refused, taking a cup of cider instead. The lass with yellow tresses carved him an ample slice of pork, and presented it on a piece of wheaten bread. Lars wolfed it down, trailing meaty juices down his chin.

Wherever this place might be, he decided, it was better than where he'd been. Fearsome adventures or no, he hadn't felt as good in two long years, since the Churchers had brought him to life. By God, these were real folk, like those of the Corps itself. There were no bloody Sisters or pinch-faced priests roaming about, ready to say do this and not that.

"Lars, by damn, it's *you!* Why, you're the last person I ever expected to see!"

Lars turned at the familiar voice, dropped the cider and choked on his meat. One of the girls pounded his back. The other found a cup of water and set it in his hands. Lars waved it away and stared in disbelief.

"Will Travers—Good *God*, man, what are you *doing* in this place! H-how in hell did you *get* here!"

Will grinned and brushed his grizzly chin. "I was about to ask you the same. Strangest damn thing I ever saw."

The girls glanced curiously at Lars. Lars clutched Will by the arm and drew him aside. "Uh, look, Will," he said, trying hard to maintain his calm, "just—tell me one thing, all right? Where are we, where *is* this place and how did we get here?"

Will shrugged. "I haven't the slightest idea, Lars. Guess it never occurred to me to ask." He winked at the flaxen-haired girl. "Havin' too much fun to care."

"You haven't—you really don't know?"

"Well what's so peculiar in that? You go lots of places and do lots of strange things. Don't have to put a *name* to it all, do you?"

"Wait, just hold on, Will." Lars was getting more and more confused by the minute. "Are you—are you trying to tell me you do this all the time?"

"Sure I do." Will looked puzzled, then broke into

a grin. " 'Cept *you* were never in 'em before, that's for certain. Damnedest thing I ever saw."

"I was never in *what*, Will?"

"In any of my dreams. Never saw you or anyone I knew." He scratched the side of his jaw. "How you suppose it works?"

Lars' mouth fell open. "That's where you think you are? In a *dream?*"

Will gave him a sour look. "No, Lars, I'm in a pig sty west of Citadel. Where the hell does it look like I am?"

For a heart-stopping instant, Lars wondered if Will was right. Could it truly be a dream? Ham and the tavern and John-William and all? Lars shook the thought away. It was far too real to be a dream. Besides, whoever heard of stalking about in another man's sleep?

Still, if it wasn't a dream, what was it? He and Will were somewhere, for sure. A place where the season was wrong, and the folk around them anything but Churchers.

"You, uh—do this all the time, do you?" Lars asked, facing Will again. "Come here, and other places as well?"

"Certainly I do," Will snapped. "Damn it all, Lars Haggart, stop lookin' at me like that!"

"Like what, Will?"

"Like I was daft or something is what." He raised a corner of his mouth in a wicked grin. "If I am, what's that make you?"

"You've surely got a point. I can't argue that."

"Hell, why argue at all?" Will jerked a thumb over his shoulder. "You don't see any sour-faced folk 'round here, do you?"

"No, I can't say as I do."

"Won't, either," Will said flatly. He shot Lars a sly wink. "I think young Felicia's got her eyes on you, boy. She's the one with hair slick as summer. 'Course if you don't like her there's—"

Will stopped as someone shouted past the green. People looked at one another, then hurriedly made their way toward the river. Lars exchanged a look with Will and they followed. A crowd of folk were gathered at the bank, craning their necks to see.

"Don't like the looks of that," said one.

"They've got no business here," grumbled another. "Trouble's what it is."

Lars edged his way through and squinted across the water. Men lined the shore, some on mounts and some afoot. Lars recognized them at once. "God's Eyes, it's them," he said tightly. "How in hell did they follow me here?"

A man Will Traver's age looked up at his words. "They're after you, are they? You've seen that bunch before?"

"Earlier," Lars told him. "They chased me and damned near caught me."

The old man made a face. "That's bad. They've got no business on King's Side of the river, that's the law. On the other hand, we got no right over *there*."

"Just what are you trying to say?" asked Lars.

"What I'm saying is, if you been crossin' their lands, they got the right to come and get you."

"Now wait," Lars protested, "how was I to know? I don't even know where I am now—much less where I was this morning!"

"Tell *them* that," Will said darkly. "Here the bastards come. . . ."

The crowd shrank back with cries of alarm, and fled to the safety of the trees. Lars stood at the river and stared. Mounts and men splashed toward him through the shallows. Mail armor and lances of iron sparked the sun.

"I got an idea you and me better wake up fast," Will muttered. "Likely save these folks a lot of trouble."

"What?" Lars looked blank. "Will, what you are talking about?"

Will closed his eyes tight and set his jaw. A lance buried itself in the bank, and then another. "Oh, no, not without me you don't!" cried Lars. He leaped at Will and held on as the river and the sky and the warriors disappeared.

Will sat up straight in bed, blinked, and stared in disbelief at Lars tangled in his arms.

"By God, get *off* me, you shameless sod," he shouted in anger. "I'll not have that kind of business under my blanket!"

SIXTEEN

It was still a good two hours till the dawn when he rousted them out of their beds—Carilee and Maureen and young Sean. They shuffled into the small common room off the kitchen, bleary-eyed with sleep. Will was already there. Amian Morse was absent. Eric, Lars' other lieutenant, had died in the demon battle.

"I'd like Morse to be here," said Lars. "I know how he feels about me, but he's still an officer in the Corps."

"He won't come, Captain," said Sean. "I tried like you asked. He, uh—"

"He says you can do what you like to him, Lars," Carilee finished. "You've nothing to say he wants to hear."

Lars felt the color rise to his cheeks. "Amian Morse is right. I've no excuse for what I did. When I face the man I'll say it straight to his face. Now is that plain enough? What I've got to say's more important than Amain Morse or any other I've offended." No one looked his way or deigned to answer. He stood and spread his hands upon the table.

"What I'm going to tell you's daft, but it's God's

truth all the same. If you don't believe me, trust Will." His frown disappeared, and a wry grin touched the corners of his mouth. "In spite of your saintly faces, I have to tell you that you're *not* sleeping souls from God's Bosom, or anything of the sort. The good Brothers and Sisters can think what they like, but it simply isn't so. I've *been* to where we're from, and so has Will. It's a real and solid world, and I'm bound to say it's a finer one than this."

For a moment, they met his words with silence, then all began shouting at once.

"Just *listen*," said Lars, raising a hand for quiet. "I'll start at the beginning, or near enough." He told them of his drunken jump into town, then the next from Ham's quarters to the place where time had come to a halt. He saw their faces when he spoke of John-William and Elaine, and the other Drifters they'd lost. Young Sean choked off a cry when he heard the words. Hope and joy brushed his features, then faded just as quickly to pain and despair.

"They're alive," said Lars. "I can't say if they're lost forever or not. I simply don't know that, Sean."

"*You* got out," the boy blurted. "That means there's a way to bring 'em back!"

"Sean, don't," Maureen said softly, and laid a gentle hand upon his arm.

Lars went on, telling them quickly of his meeting with Will, and what had gone before. "I *know* I've been there before," he said firmly. "I felt as if I'd remember it all in a moment. Only a moment more." He grinned and draped his arm over Will Travers' shoulder. "Will's the key to it all—Will, and Ham's corn ale. Though I'd strongly recommend Will's way against the other."

He jammed his hands in his belt, and gave the

floor a thoughtful stare. "You see it now, don't you? Will here thought it was all a dream. He'd no idea he was jumping, for he was convinced he shared no talents with the Corps. Instead it seems he's a power that fair puts us all to shame. Those fine tales he's been a'spinning are a good deal more than that."

"God's Eyes, Will . . ." Carilee shook her head in wonder. "Fair maids and palaces, and animals with noses like snakes. I thought you were makin' it all up!"

"So did I," Will said wearily.

Lars looked at the others. "You see what it means, do you not? We're not stuck here on Harmony forever. There are worlds out there without number, including one that's our own."

"So what are you saying," Sean said testily, "we dream or get drunk, and go where we like? Is that it, Lars? Or get ourselves caught in some place where the minutes never pass!"

"None of those at all," said Lars. "Or maybe a bit of all three, for that matter. It's not dreaming or ale that sent Will and me wanderin' about. It's a—a different way of looking at a jump. Least that's the way I'm thinking."

"Jumping's just jumping," said Sean. "If there's another way to do it, I'm damned if I know what it is."

"I think *I* do . . ." said Carilee.

"You think you do what?" Lars gave her a narrow look. Something in her voice, the way the light touched her eyes, was not to his liking at all.

"Why, I don't know for certain. Not really." She glanced up and smiled. "Something, though. Something I get to feeling sometimes. Like you said, I guess. A different way of thinking . . . bein' some-where else."

"Or not thinking at all," Will broke in. "That's the state of dreaming, is it not? And too much drinking's the same."

"Exactly," said Lars. "That's what I'm trying to say, only I don't know how to say it."

"You won't, either," Will snorted. "For it's nothing to do with words."

"But it's *there*, damn it, Will. And something in our heads knows how to get there, too. We've got to learn what it is!" He paced the small room, a storm above his brow. "Let's take it from the start if we can. This Brother Jerome, now, we know nothing about him at all, and likely never will. They say he worked his magic from something he found aboard the vessel that brought them here—the thing that's buried now 'neath Citadel. Whatever he did it worked—and what would he say we were but sleeping souls—the shades of God's Unborn? I'm sure it's what he believed; it's the way a Churcher thinks."

"And *we've* no memory of what we were," Maureen reminded him.

"This place that you and Will saw was where we lived?" Carilee said wistfully. "You truly think that's so?"

"I do, Carilee. I feel most strongly that it is." He glanced at Will, and Will nodded assent.

"There's a thing left out of all this," Sean said tightly. "Demons are jumpers, too. And Brother Jerome didn't pull *them* out of his hat. They've been here from the beginning, before we ever appeared."

"I know they have, Sean. And I can't give you an answer. I've no idea what they are, or what they've to do with us." He paused, then, and knew that this

135

was the time, that he had to tell them the rest. "During the battle," he said quietly, "I *saw* something out there. At the time, I thought my mind was playing tricks. Sister-Major sensed I knew something I didn't want to tell. I said there was nothing at all. Even then, I guess I knew it was half a lie. After what's happened since, I know I didn't imagine what I saw."

Lars waited, searching for the words to make it work. "When we jumped the bowmen over and loosed our bolts, I knew we had them. It was a move that took them completely by surprise. I *saw* them, damn it—screaming and dyin' as our missles ripped their ranks. It wasn't something I simply *wanted* to happen, it did! And then—all of a sudden, it wasn't so at all. That moment was erased and another took its place. This time, the demons were gone before our bolts could ever touch 'em. What I saw in less than a blink was *something that could have happened and didn't!*"

Sean, Carilee and Maureen looked at him and stared. Will, somehow, didn't seem surprised. "God's Witness," he rasped, "it's true. They're always a hairthin faster, always a blink ahead!"

"The demons know something we don't," Lars went on. "They can be where they like a second faster—know where we're going and jump to meet us."

"That's not possible!" Sean snorted.

"It is," said Maureen, "God help us, Sean it is."

"They saw us jump and catch them cold," said Lars. "Then they—froze that instant and got away. And when we jumped back to safety behind our lines, they knew exactly where we'd be. My God, Sean—they were *waiting* there for us, were they not?"

"That's freezin' more than a second," muttered Will. "We attacked the regular jumpers. It was the *long*jumpers came after us."

Lars spread his hands. "I hope you're not asking me how it's done, for I haven't the slightest idea. I only know it happened. We've got the dead to prove it," he added grimly.

Carilee shook her head. "Lars, the Mazefield stops them. They get slaughtered all the time. Why can't they—*see* the snares and traps and get away?"

"Because the snares and traps aren't alive," Lars said at once.

"What?"

"I don't know, Carilee, but I'm certain that's the reason." He was just as startled as the others at his answer. It came to him without thought or reason.

"Maybe they can read us," Maureen said with a chill. "Do you think that could be?"

Lars wanted to tell her she was wrong. It was likely, though, she'd brushed the edge of the truth. "Whatever it is they do, there's some sort of limit, thank God. If there wasn't they'd put time to their use for more than a second, would they not? What if it was three instead of one—or maybe four? With that much advantage, there'd be no way to stop 'em. And they *can* be killed. They're not invincible, Praise God."

"They're not far from it," muttered Sean.

Lars studied the young man a long moment. If he didn't set Sean aright soon, he'd have another Amian Morse on his hands.

"And all we've said, then, all we've put together," asked Will, "what's the good of it, Lars?"

Lars looked at him without expression. "Let's think on it," he said, "and get together later in the day.

We've a lot to consider all at once." He glanced at Sean and Maureen and Carilee. "For now all this is only among ourselves. The others need to know, but I'd like to give 'em answers instead of questions."

And how do you figure on doing that? he asked himself.

By late afternoon, Lars learned Jeffrey had taken a bold step in his efforts to shame the Corps and bring himself closer to power. Nearly a regiment of Churcher troops surrounded the walls, blowing horns and rattling iron, and shouting loudly at whoever cared to listen. Neither Lars not any other in the barracks paid them heed, but the townsfolk were greatly impressed—and that, indeed, was Jeffrey's sole intention.

Only one matter greatly concerned Lars, and that was a glimpse of Jeffrey from the roof. From his dress he'd clearly risen overnight from priestly aide to Sister-Major, to the exalted rank of Brother-Major himself. Whatever that might mean, Lars knew it couldn't bode well for Sister-Major. Or anyone else for that matter. In spite of himself he cared for the leathery old warrior. It pained him to think Jeffrey had somehow put her in danger.

"What d'you think he'll do?" asked Carilee. She sat cross-legged in the window of the loft, chewing hard bread and combing her hair.

"Likely nothing at all," Lars told her. "The show's not for us, it's for the rabble. So everyone'll know that he can do it."

That wasn't entirely true, but he didn't mention that to Carilee. Since he'd learned the priest was mad as frogs are green, Lars had been less hurried to sell him short. The troopers were here for show, but there was much more to it than that.

"What are you thinking," Carilee asked of a sudden, "what you'll do with what you know?"

"It's not simply *me*," he corrected. "I can't make a decision like that. Not for the whole Corps itself. Besides, it's not as if I had any answers at the moment."

"But if you did?" she persisted.

"If I did," he sighed, "I'd see the last of this pesthole, Carilee. Take you and all the rest back to where it is we belong. I'd like to remember who I was and what I did. I'd like to think about me as a lad and—Damn it all I'd like to *know* if I've got a mother or if I came from under a rock!"

Carilee grinned. "Of course you've got a mother."

"And how would you know that?"

"You do, that's all."

Lars went to her and took her shoulders, a wicked smile on his face.

"Since you know so much, O'Farr, tell me this. How do you know you're not my *sister* 'stead of my lover? And who's to say you've not a fine fat husband waitin' patient to take you back? Tell me that, now?"

Carilee's eyes went wide. "A—a husband? A *fat* husband, Lars?"

"Aye, fat and mean to boot. And half a dozen brats in the bargain."

"I don't," Carilee said crossly. "And I'm not your sister, either."

"Prove that you're not then, girl. A sister'd never—"

"Just *stay* away from me," she warned. Bright flecks of green sparked her eyes. "I'm—I'm still out of pleasure with you."

"God's Eyes. How long's *that* going to last?"

"Maybe forever. I'm not quite certain."

"I hope it's shorter than that."

Carilee looked away. "Would you, Lars? Truly? Leave right now if you could?"

"Why in the world would I not?"

"Well they need us here, don't they?"

Lars looked astonished. "God's Witness, we don't owe them a thing," he said sharply, "not a thing, O'Farr. Who do you think got us *into* this mess in the first place?"

"Just asking is all," Carilee sighed. She glanced past Lars to the west, the blood-red of the sun dancing off her amber hair. "You're right, I guess. There's not a lot we can do here anyway, is there? I mean, unless we learn to jump as well as demons. And even if we don't, we've still got to learn just *how* to get back to where we're from. The way things are with the war, we'd better learn to do *some*thing real fast, wouldn't you say?"

Lars looked pained. "Will you stop talking long enough to tell me what you're saying?"

"I don't know," she said absently. "Maybe nothing at all. I was just wondering, though, Lars. . . ."

"Yes?"

"In your talking you never mentioned it at all. If we're not the Unborn, and God didn't give us the powers and talents we've got—where *did* they come from? The way you tell it, we're just common folk jerked out of another world. Did the people you and Will saw have the power? Did you see anyone *jump?*"

Lars' mouth fell open. For some reason, the question had never occurred to him at all. "No, no, I saw nothing of the sort."

"Well, then," Carilee sighed, "maybe that's the answer, Lars. You don't just—magically pull people from other worlds who have powers. Folks get powers *because* you pull 'em through. I'm probably wrong, of course, but—"

"Great God," said Lars, staring at her in disbelief. "When am I going to learn what a wonder you are. Why, that's the way it *has* to be, Carilee!"

SEVENTEEN

Before the dark set in, Lars checked the guards he'd placed about the roof and on the grounds. It was a gesture and little else, for he was certain Brother Jeffrey would do no more than he was doing— march around the walls and make noise. Still, it made his folk feel useful. More than that, it let them know he was still in command. Apparently, there'd been some question of that.

"You can't truly blame 'em," Will had told him. "Everybody lost someone in the fight. They're mad and full of sorrow all at once. It's not you they hate, Lars Haggart. It's what happened, and not being able to fight back."

"They've got the right to blame me," Lars said tightly. "I was running the show."

"Sean and Amian are just as responsible as you. They shouldn't have let the demons bait them."

Which has nothing to do with the matter, thought Lars. *Will's missed the point. Amian's a hero because he dashed headlong into the fray. And I'm a villain because I hit him for being a fool. . . .*

And Morse and Sean were doing their best to make damn sure no one forgot.

*   *   *

Lars heard the guards shout, and peered out the window of the loft. Torches lit the gate where a white flag waved from a pole. "Let 'em in," Lars called down, "but no farther than the middle of the yard."

When Lars arrived, Jeffrey's men were making a show of looking grim and ready for battle. There were six Churcher troopers, a Captain and a sergeant. The sergeant held a torch, and the Captain gripped a rolled piece of paper in his fist. When Lars appeared he looked up quickly and snapped to attention.

"You are Captain Lars Haggart, of the Arm of God Regiment of Mother Church?"

"Get on with it," Lars said with a yawn.

The Captain flushed and unfolded his message. "Captain Lars Haggart is hereby ordered and instructed to present himself without delay of any sort to the Captain of Mother Church Guards at the first hour of dawning; from there to be escorted to Citadel for urgent counsel with War Board officers of the Holy Virgin Mother Anne Marie. This directive is signed and so ordered by Brother-Major Jeffrey of the Holy Order of Arms of Mother Church." The Captain rolled his paper into a tube and offered it to Lars.

"I think I can remember," said Lars. "That's all, is it?"

"I'm to wait for your answer," the Captain said stiffly.

"Good. Wait all night if you're inclined."

The Churcher glared and set his teeth, barked an order and brought his men full about. A soldier in the rear glanced over his shoulder, and shot a wink at Lars.

143

"The arch past the tavern in half an hour," he hissed. "Be there for certain!"

"What?" Lars came alert. "For God's sake, man—" The trooper was out of sight, but Lars knew at once that it was Ham. He looked curiously after his friend, then turned back to the barracks.

"You're not going," Will said flatly. "Counsel with War Board officers, my bloody toe. What kind of fool does Jeffrey take you for, Lars?"

"I've not much choice, now do I?"

"The hell you don't!" He grabbed Lars' arm and held him back. "You going to tell me what's about, or keep it to yourself?"

"Tell you what, Will?"

"God's Breath, will you stop it? That priest with a lemon in his mouth has got himself promoted. That didn't seem to surprise you this afternoon, and I guess I'm wondering why."

"Nothing surprises me anymore. Does it you?"

The answer didn't satisfy Will, but it was clear Lars had nothing more to say. Muttering to himself, he left Lars in the yard and stomped inside.

Lars appeared in shadow, glanced quickly about and gave a deep sigh of relief. There was no reason the jump shouldn't have taken him where it did. However, the taste of his last 'venture was still sour in his mouth. Something moved across the way and Lars tensed. Ham slipped along the wall and came up beside him.

"Every time you pops in and out like that it shivers my back," he complained. "I'll never get used to the business, for sure."

"Sorry," Lars said shortly. "Next time I'll march

through town with drums and horns. Now. What the *hell* is this about? What am I doing here?"

"You're here 'cause someone wants to see you."

"And who might that someone be?"

"I can't rightly say. Whoever it is is damned important. I know because they—"

"God's Eyes Ham." Lars stepped back and stared. "You don't *know* who it is?"

Ham's rodent beak began to twitch. "No," he said sharply, "I don't. But I trust the person who gave me my instructions. I guessed you'd trust me the same."

"All right," Lars sighed. He could find no answer to that. "I do trust you, Ham. But you know what's happening back at the barracks. I've a right to be some cautious, you'll admit."

"Sure you do. And cautious is what we'll be. The house you want's over there. Across the street and up the stairs. Where the candle's in the window. I'll be waiting down here."

"Fine," said Lars, giving the darkened streets a dubious eye. "And how's your lovely wife since last we met?"

Ham grinned in delight. "Docile as a hare, Praise God, thanks to you. Every time she raises her voice I simply tell her I'll call the demon up again. Fair shuts her up fast, it does."

"I'm pleased to be of service," said Lars.

The stairs were narrow, and creaked with every step. The sound set his teeth on edge, though he knew it didn't matter about the noise. Any assassin with half his wits could close his eyes and loose a bolt and hit him square.

The door was directly at the top of the stairs. Lars grasped the knob and turned it slowly, kicked the panel open and went flat, blade in his hand at the ready.

"Now there's *no* need for that," the voice said softly. "I mean you no harm, Lars Haggart. . . ."

Lars went rigid. "H—Holy Mother, is that you?"

Anne Marie laughed, a sound sweet and clear as silver bells. "Why, I'm near to certain it's me. Aren't you, Captain?"

Lars tried to find his voice. She sat on a bench by the window, head tossed back to show a tumble of raven hair. The light from the room's single candle turned her face the color of gold. Lars had thought her lovely beyond all measure when they'd met. Seeing her now in such a setting, he could believe there was a heavenly quality about her. She seemed a flickering vision instead of flesh, a lucent creature of such perfection she could scarce endure for long so base a world.

"Captain," Anne Marie said gently, "you are *staring* at me, I believe."

"No, I—" Lars cleared his throat. "It's just that I am most surprised to find you here, Mother."

"Well . . . I don't suppose I blame you for that."

"And where's the Good Sister of the Veil? I, uh— don't see her around."

"That's because she's not here," Anne Marie laughed. "Goodness, the poor dear can scarcely move. It wouldn't be seemly to drag her about in the night, now would it?"

"No, I don't suppose it would." Lars framed his words with care. "On the other hand, there might be some who'd say it's not seemly at all for Holy Mother to go flitting about in the dark. Alone, no less, and in the company of a—a man of less than pious persuasion."

"Less than pious persuasion are you, now?" Anne Marie hid a girlish laugh behind her hand. "I'd say that's quite a good description. Considering your behavior—or the lack of it, perhaps—in the tavern of the Celibate Priest."

Lars raised a brow. "Ah, you know about that, do you. That explains your acquaintance with Ham." *And what else, perhaps? Ham's acquaintance with Jeffrey? Treacheries a girl of such innocence could never fathom?*

"Oh, no, not really." Anne Marie shook her head. "I'm not acquainted with Ham, nor does he have the slightest idea who you're meeting. Others, though, who tell me things that occur, know of Ham's acquaintance with *you*." She paused, then, and considered him a moment. "Does it concern you all that much, Lars Haggart? That I'd break the rules and speak to you direct?" She frowned, then, an expression far too old for her girlish years. "I *make* the rules, you know. I don't see why I can't break them if I like."

"Why, no reason at all," said Lars.

"And I *did* need to see you. On a most urgent matter."

"I gathered that it was, Holy Mother."

She stood, then, coming gracefully to her feet. "Besides, it's not the—not the same as talking to just *any* man, is it? We discussed this before and I've given it a great deal of thought. You're scarcely wholly mortal, Lars Haggart. You're more like—well, more like *me*, as a fact. A spiritual being, clothed in mortal form. It's not as if I'm talking to a man born in sin. You *do* come from the Holy Bosom of God!"

"Yes, in a—in a sense, I suppose we all do," Lars said absently.

"What, Captain?"

"Nothing, really. Just a poor bit of philosophy rattling about, Holy Mother."

Anne Marie stared through the dirt-encrusted window, then turned and faced him again. "We've much to talk about and very little time, Lars Haggart. There's another bench if you'd care to sit."

"I'm fine, Mother, but thanks."

Anne Marie remained afoot herself. "I'm sorry for your losses in the field. It was a terrible thing indeed. Please know I pray for those departed."

"I'm grateful that you do."

"Captain. . . . This business of you and Brother Jeffrey in the morning. . . ." She met his eyes then glanced quickly away. "I'm troubled about this. Most troubled, indeed."

"To be honest, so am I," said Lars. He moved a step nearer then stopped. "If you're troubled, as you say, I'd guess you have a reason. Is it because you know what Jeffrey has in mind? Or perhaps because you don't?"

"I don't think I understand, Lars Haggart."

Lars wondered just how heavy he dared to tread. "Do you—question Jeffrey's intentions for any reason? Is that what you're saying?"

Anne Marie looked puzzled. "Why, no—why on earth would I do that?"

"I've no idea," Lars lied. "But you did just say you were worried 'bout my meeting in the morning. I thought perhaps you wondered what it was for—and Jeffrey wouldn't say."

"I said nothing of the sort!" she snapped, tossing back her hair. "I haven't *asked* Good Jeffrey. I would never insult him by doing such a thing. I am *troubled,* Captain Haggart, because there is clearly some sort of—of *conflict* between you and Jeffrey, and Jeffrey and Sister-Major. I don't know what it is and I don't like it. And I can tell you right now that *God* doesn't care much for it, either."

"He doesn't?"

Anne Marie's eyes met his. "No, Lars Haggart, he does not. This world was called Harmony for a reason. Because that's the kind of home He wanted us to have. He is grieved, I can tell you, that we've not met the test he set before us, that we've still not defeated the Devil's own. And to argue among ourselves when we most desperately need to fight in fellowship and love. . . ."

"Have you talked to Sister-Major about this?"

"About what?"

"Uh, disharmony and such. The lack of love in the fight against Evil."

"Why no, of course I haven't." Anne Marie looked blank. "I hope you're not implying I'd speak to one and not the other about this? That I'd pit the Sons and Daughters of God against each other?" She shook her head sternly at Lars. "I'm shocked, really, that you'd ask such a thing. What kind of Holy Mother do you think I am?"

"Mother, please—" Lars rolled his eyes at the ceiling. "I'm sorry, and I hope it doesn't offend you too greatly, but I think it's time we laid a few truths on the table. I *know* Brother Jeffrey's managed to set Sister-Major aside. And that greatly troubles *me*, I can tell you. Sister-Major trusts me, and I trust her. I do not trust Jeffrey, and he definitely does not like me. Mother, whether you like it or not I'm going to say it. I *don't* think it would soil your Holy Self too much if you'd spend a bit more time on earthly matters. Keeping your hands *out* of this business isn't helping any at all."

Anne Marie looked as if he'd struck her. Her dark eyes went wide and she grasped the wall to keep from falling. "You cannot—talk to me like this," she cried. "I am God's Voice on Harmony, Lars Haggart!"

"Good," Lars said shortly. "Then you'd best tell *Him* we're in big trouble down here." Anne Marie opened her mouth to protest. Lars stopped her with a gesture. "Just wait, Mother. I've started, so hear me out. I respect you greatly, but I don't pretend to understand you. You went to a great deal of trouble to meet me in secret. I'm afraid I can't guess the reason why. You're the Virgin Mother Anne Marie. You don't *have* to do things like this, and yet you did. And now that you have, you refuse to look the issues square in the face. All you ever do is talk in circles!"

"I have summoned you half a dozen times since the battle," she said coolly. "You chose to ignore me, Lars Haggart. It seems I—I *have* to resort to trickery to get your attention."

"No. Now that's not so and you know it. You didn't want anyone else to know we were meeting. Yet, now that I'm here you're doing everything you can to keep from talking about things that *need* talking about. You just keep—oh, now, don't do that, please!"

Anne Marie's full lips trembled; a veritable river of silver tears rolled down her cheeks. Lars wanted to cut out his heart. Anyone who'd hurt such a lovely and fragile creature. . . .

"Mother, I'm sorry. I never meant to bring you to that."

"No, don't. . . ." She shook her head in anguish.

"I was—I was wrong. I've been a terrible fool, Lars Haggart. Worse than that, I've committed the sin of pride. I let myself believe things I had no right to believe."

Lars shook his head. "I'm sorry. I don't understand."

"You don't remember, do you? You don't remember at all."

"Remember what? God's Witness, what is it I'm supposed to remember?"

"What—what we talked about before."

"Before? You mean, when we met at Citadel?"

"Yes, of course." She sniffed and rubbed her sleeve across her face. "Don't you *know* why I asked you here? Truly? I have prayed, Lars Haggart, asking for the truth. God was good enough to give me an answer and—and I assumed He might have done the same for you. I see, now, that isn't so. But of course that *doesn't* change the truth revealed to me." She stood straight and looked him in the eye. There was just a touch of moisture on her lips. "Come here, Lars Haggart. You're standing much too far away for this."

"For—for what, Mother?" Lars' heart began to hammer against his chest.

"For what I have to say. What you *must* hear me say." She held out her hands and motioned him forward. Lars took a step and stopped. "I told you before," she said calmly, "that I have given much thought to the question of sin. Especially the sin of carnal knowledge. You remember that, don't you?"

"Oh, yes. Yes, I certainly do. . . ."

"Well, then. I won't bore you with the theology behind my thinking. You're not a religious scholar, Lars Haggart, and it would simply go over your head. What I'm saying is that God's Word on the matter is exactly as I suspected. As Holy Mother, I'm quite beyond the vale of sin. I mean, you simply can't be in a state of Grace all the time and be a sinner as well. It doesn't make sense, does it? And as for you—why, you're no more a mortal than I am, really. You crossed the bridge of death to wait for incarnation. And you *weren't* born again. Brother Jerome brought you here instead. That's the key to the whole thing." She looked at Lars and stepped closer. Her hands touched his and slid lightly to his shoulders. Lars felt as if two burning brands had found his flesh.

"You see what I'm saying?" she whispered. "We're incapable of lust, Lars Haggart. Whatever—knowledge, we might have of one another would be a blessing, a pure and lovely meeting of your spirit and mine. Our union might appear to be clothed in fleshly passion, but in truth it would be nothing of the sort."

"Mother . . . Anne Marie, look—" Lars gripped her hands and held her away. "I, uh—know you think you know what you think. That is, you think you know that I. That you—"

"Hush, Lars. . . ." She pressed a soft finger to his lips. "I'm your spiritual adviser on this world. I ought to know what's best for you, now shouldn't I?"

"Yes, I suppose that's so. Still. . . ."

Her eyes closed and her fingers laced gently behind his neck. Her tender form pressed against him, fearfully at first, then bolder and bolder still.

"You'll have to show me," she said softly. "I don't know what to do."

"What?"

Her eyes came open again. "Lars, I know absolutely nothing about carnal desire. Or *spiritual* carnal desire, as it were. I assume we'll do whatever we would do if we were mortal. I mean, it'll probably *seem* like the same thing, won't it? Only I haven't the slightest idea what that is."

"You—you're off to a real good start," Lars assured her.

"Oh, well fine. Show me what comes next."

Lars knew he shouldn't. He thought of at least a hundred sound reasons why not. None of them seemed important with the fresh smell of her hair assailing his senses, her parted lips scarce an inch from his own. He wrapped his arms about her, and brought her to him and kissed her. Gently, at first, then fiercely as a sigh escaped her throat and her body began to shudder. Her fingers left his neck and wandered into his hair. His heart beat like thunder in his ears. It sounded as if a herd of great beasts were pounding across the earth. He kissed her again. The sound grew louder still. . . .

Lars grabbed her arms and pushed her roughly away. Anne Marie flushed and looked startled. The thunder came closer, pounding up the narrow stairs then crashing against the door.

Lars jumped. . . .

He stood in the center of the loft and caught his breath. The press of her body was still sweet.

Ham, you little rodent, if you sold me out and led them to me, I swear to God I'll have your head . . . !

"Lars!"

"What?" Lars jerked about and came to his senses. Will Travers poked his head into the loft.

"Where in hell have you been, man? Never mind, Praise God you're here. Come on—hurry!"

"Will, what is it, what's wrong?"

"It's Carilee," he said darkly. "You'd best come quick. I think she's starting to Drift. . . ."

EIGHTEEN

He held her close against him, cradling her head to his chest. Her hair was damp and limp, all the body gone. It clung to the flesh of his arm like pale weeds under water. He brushed a strand from her cheek, and gently wiped the bright beads of moisture from her brow.

"You've got to fight it," he whispered. "You can't give in, Carilee. You mustn't let that happen!"

She found him with her eyes and tried to smile. "I'm trying, Lars . . . I truly am . . . I'm so very very tired. . . ."

"I know, Carilee."

"I—lied, you know. I could feel it tryin' to take me. I didn't want you to know."

"You should have, love. We're not to have secrets, remember? Yes . . . yes, that's so."

She felt so light, so incredibly light in his arms, as if a part of her was already gone. *My God, no—it's too soon for that, much much too soon!*

"Carilee, look at me. *Look* at me, O'Farr."

"Yes. Yes, Lars." Her eyes were much too bright, green as deep deep water, hard as polished stone.

He knew they mirrored a light that only Carilee could see.

"No, damn it," he said sharply, "don't look out there look at *me!*" Carilee stared past him and mouthed his name. Lars took a deep breath and slapped her hard. His palm stung her cheeks and left its mark. He hit her again and again, the blows snapping her head from side to side.

"Lars, for God's sake," cried Will, "what's the good of that!"

Carilee groaned and tried to jerk herself free. Lars pulled her roughly to him and struck her again. This time her eyes opened wide and turned on him in a fury.

"That's it," Lars said to himself. "That's the way, love." He reached for a jug of cold water and dashed it in her face.

Carilee choked and sputtered. "Stop it," she screamed. "Leave me alone, damn you!" Lars slapped her again and the blow sent her reeling. She cried out and covered her face.

Lars stood and tried to keep his hands from shaking. Curious faces peered into the room. Lars turned angrily and shouted them out. "We should've thought of this before," he said grimly. "We didn't know what Driftin' was—we sat about with our fingers in our noses and let them go."

Will frowned. "And you think this'll stop her? Hurting the lass like that?"

"You're damned right I do," Lars said firmly. He glanced at Carilee and back to Will. "Unless I miss my guess, we named it proper for sure. *Drifting*, Will—by God, that's exactly what it is. Jumping's going from one place to the next—across the room, or back to another world. Drifting's getting caught in between, like poor John-William and the rest."

"Why, though?" Will wet his lips. "Why Carilee and John-William, and maybe a dozen more?"

Lars shrugged. "I'll tell you what I think, but I can't prove it's so. I felt it out there, Will. Something like a—a cord, trying to pull me on. We don't belong here, we belong back there. At that place beside the river." He nodded at Carilee. "That's what's happening to her. The cord wants her back. Only you can't *get* back if you Drift. All you do's get caught in the middle."

"*You* didn't," said Will. "You were there and you got away."

"I didn't get there Drifting, now did I?" Lars slammed a fist into his palm. "Damn it all, Will, we've got to find the answer. If we don't, we'll be stuck on this demon-cursed world the rest of our lives. Which can't be overly long, the way the war is going. Carilee hit it, I'm next to certain. We know how to jump *because we jumped*. Period. The talent comes from crossing over. We did it, Will, you and I. That means we can do it again—and teach the others as well."

Will rubbed a hand across his jaw. "Have you— tried again, Lars? Have you tried to go back since we returned?"

"No," Lars said too quickly, "I haven't. I just—"

"—You just know you can't, right? You're scared to try, but even if you had the nerve to do it, you know it wouldn't work."

Lars looked startled. "And how—how did you know that?"

"Because I had to find out," Will said shortly.

"Pure scared the hell out of me, too, I'll tell you that."

"You tried to go back? Back to where we were?"

"Awake and out of the dream. Nothing happened, Lars. Nothing except a—real peculiar feeling."

"What kind of a feeling?"

Will gave him a wary look. "I think you'd best see that for yourself. I mean that, Lars. I think you'd better know."

Lars' mouth went dry. "God's Breath, I don't think I *want* to know, Will. I'm not shamed to say it— you've got more nerve than I."

"Or less to lose," Will muttered. "Go on, just do it. You're goin' to have to know, and there's no way I can tell it. Just imagine the place we were. Try to go there again."

Lars glanced at Carilee. She was sleeping soundly for the moment—a gentle, quiet sleep, nothing akin to Drifting. "You'd best be right, old man, or I'll never speak to you again."

"That's the bloody truth," Will grinned.

Lars closed his eyes. He saw the flowing river, willows bowed above the water, a clear blue sky flecked with clouds. For a whisper of a moment he thought he was there, that Will was wrong and the jump had worked. He was home, back home where he belonged!

With no warning at all, the terrible numbing fear reached out and took him in its grasp. It was a thing so awesome, so sudden and unrelenting, Lars cried out aloud and fled for his life. . . .

"God's Holy Witness. . . ." He stared at Will and took a shaky breath. "What—what the hell *was* that!"

"Some kind of a presence," Will said flatly.

"Something that knows you're there. It barred the way and wouldn't let you pass."

"Yes. Yes, that's exactly what it was."

"Something's out there, Lars, guarding the way. It knows we want by, and it's not about to let us." Will Travers suddenly looked a great deal older than he was. "We're not any closer to gettin' home—hell, we're a lot farther off, you ask me. Whatever it is out there—it won't even let me dream anymore."

Lars worked with her through the night. Whenever she started to Drift, he slapped her until she cried, tossed cold water in her face and shouted curses in her ears. Carilee fought him with a will—hurt turning to anger, and back to pain and tears. Lars was satisfied as long as she kicked and screamed. When she sagged in his arms and her eyes began to glaze, he did things to her that he didn't care to remember. The very flesh he'd touched so gently in his loving he now abused. Carilee shrieked until her voice was a ragged cry and nothing more.

Once, in spite of all he could do he nearly lost her. Her body began to flicker, fade like a guttering flame. For an instant he saw her floating in the place with no time, soundlessly calling his name. Cursing himself for what he did, he brought her back with a vengeance.

"I'm hungry, Lars. I'm hungry and thirsty and—my God, I hurt all over!"

Lars started, laughed like a madman and covered her with kisses. Carilee winced at his touch and he drew away.

"Lars, you—you're crying," she said. "Don't, love, I'm all right. Really I am."

"Are you?" he asked anxiously. "Truly, Carilee? You're not—"

"No, I am *not* Drifting," she said firmly. "I thought I was last night and you were gone and I was scared. Now, though—Lars, what happened? I remember some but not a lot."

"Good. I'll explain it all later. Remembering's not what you need right now. Just stay right there, and I'll get you something to eat."

Carilee sat up as best she could. "Is it morning or what? The light looks kind of funny."

"It's morning or close to it."

"I've had better nights, I'll tell you that."

"So have I, for certain."

"Lars. . . ."

"What, Carilee?" He saw her eyes begin to mist and held her close.

"I had some very bad dreams. Terrible, awful things."

"Forget them now. That's all over."

"No," she said curiously, "that's not so. They're not over at all." Lars looked at her with alarm and she shook her head. "I don't mean me, it's not that. It's the things I saw. It's not over, Lars. I'm afraid it's just beginning."

"You've lost your senses," Will growled. "Whatever he wants with you, Lars, it's damned sure nothing good."

"I *know* what he wants," Lars said flatly. "He wants my hide on the wall. I don't intend to walk in and hand him a skinning knife."

"Huh!" Will grunted.

"You said it yourself once, and you were right. We can't sit here and do nothing. I know Brother Jeffrey, and I know what he'll do. That's what this meeting is all about. He'll use me to raise himself higher if he can." He shot the others a grin. "I'll take a care, Will. And I can jump back quickly enough, if that's what I need to do."

"You don't have to go alone," Carilee protested. "I'm—all right, Lars, really."

"You're not, and I need you here," Lars said shortly. He turned and let his eyes touch Sean. "It took a man to come and face me like you did. We've all made mistakes around here, Sean. You've owned up to yours and that's that."

Sean shifted his boots and looked at Lars square. "Maybe I don't see eye to eye with you, Captain. But I'll not wear my rank and mutter behind your back. That's a child's game, and I'll have no part of it anymore." He shook his head and frowned. "Amian's wrong in that. It's not the proper way, and I'm shamed I went along."

"Finished and over and done," said Lars, slapping him firmly on the shoulder. He turned, then, and his eyes went dark as night. "God's Witness, I'd like to know where Morse has taken himself. I don't like this at all."

"He's not in the barracks," said Sean. "I'll swear to that."

"He's jumped," said Carilee. "That's all he could have done."

"Where, though?" Lars said irritably. "What's he doing, hopping about the hills like a hare?" He turned on his heels and faced them all. "While I'm gone, there's a thing that needs to be done. We can't wait longer, and we owe it to the others. Get them together and tell them. Everything. All we talked about. What happened to Will and me—where we came from and who we are. Tell them what I saw in the place between, John-William and the rest. And Carilee—" He paused and gave her a smile. "Tell them there's no more Drifting. We can set that problem aside—God knows we've got enough to worry about."

"Anything else?" asked Sean.

"Yes. One thing. Tell 'em to put their heads to thinking. I want to know how to get back home 'fore we're up to our lovely bottoms in bloody demons."

A guard called out from the roof, and Lars heard a shout from the palisade wall. "That'll be the good Churchers come to March me to Citadel." He grinned and straightened his jacket and touched his blade. "Sean, tell that bastard a Captain of Karma Corps doesn't walk to where he's going like ordinary folk. Tell him if he wants me, I'm already there."

With a short explosion of air, Lars vanished.

NINETEEN

Good Brothers and Sisters gasped in alarm as Lars Haggart suddenly appeared in their midst. Lars grinned, and made no effort to hide his pleasure.

"Sorry, there's nothing more," he told them plainly. "We're all out of brimstone and fire."

Jeffrey alone retained his calm. He sat in his chair and faced Lars with no expression at all. "I half expected such a gesture, Lars Haggart. You have a habit of disrespect for Mother Church."

"None intended, I assure you," Lars said glibly. "Disrespect, I'd say, is more on the order of your lovely missive to me. *Ordered* and *instructed* to attend? Not requested, and certainly not invited."

Jeffrey wet his lips in distaste. "We didn't ask you here to listen to flowery speech."

"You didn't *ask* me here at all," Lars reminded him. "Be that as it may, why *am* I here, priest? I assume you have some reason?" Peering about the room, he saw the usual War Board members were at hand, as well as several he'd never seen. Sister-Major sat at the far end of the table. A look passed between them, a brief and telling glance that told Lars much about her condition and his own. Her features were pale and drawn, yet her eyes showed a fury held in check, a spirit still very much alive.

Jeffrey caught their exchange. "The *reason* for your summons," he said evenly, "should be as clear to you as it is to us. Your regiment suffered grievous losses, Captain Haggart. Nearly half, I believe. We share your sorrow and of course you have our prayers." Jeffrey paused and glanced to heaven. "Be that as it may, there's the matter of just *how* this tragedy came about. Whether such, ah—losses need have occurred."

"That's my responsibility," Sister-Major said shortly, "not Captain Haggart's. He merely—"

"Please, Sister. . . ." Jeffrey gave her a patient smile. "There's a point that needs making, if you will. No one doubts that you were in command. The question's whether your orders were carried out to best effect."

"And you'd know that, of course," said Lars. "Being a seasoned warrior and all."

"*My* military prowess is not at question here, Captain."

"Praise God for that."

Several Brothers and Sisters gave him nasty looks. Lars risked a glance at Sister-Major. He knew, of course, her words were meant for him and not for Jeffrey. She was telling him what he'd certainly expected to hear—that she'd back him and claim he'd acted on her orders. Jeffrey might find them both at fault, but that was a minor sin compared to the truth.

That's what he's after, Lars thought darkly. *He's guessed we made a bargain, but by God he's got to prove it . . !*

"Captain," Jeffrey said smoothly, leaning toward Lars across the table, "we seek the truth here and nothing more. There is no need to strike out at me, or any other person on the Board."

"Ah, well," Lars said with relief, "if it's truth we're after, I'm your man. Would it please the Board if I speak a bit of it now?"

"In time, Captain. Now, however—"

"—Is as good a time as any," Lars finished, coming quickly to his feet. "You want to talk about fighting, why we will," he said harshly. "I was there, by the way, with blade in hand. And so was Sister-Major. Were any of the rest of you there beside us? Did you *see* what happened out there? God's Eyes, people— who says *any*one's to blame for what happened? I've told you from the start and you wouldn't listen. The bloody demons are death comin' at you like the wind. You've been fighting them for two hundred years—why the *hell* should I have to tell you that?"

Jeffrey looked pained. "We've heard all this before, Captain Haggart."

"Well by *God*, you're hearin' it again!" Lars' eyes flashed with anger. "It's easy to sit here safe and read battles out of a book. Go out and get some blood on your saintly hands—see how *that* feels for a change!"

"Is it true or is it not, Captain Haggart, that your very own folk have shown concern for your manner of command?"

"What? What's that?" Lars was taken aback by the sudden question. He searched about the table and found the source. "Oh, yes—Brother Job, is it not?" He gave the old man a knowing smile. "Who told you such foolishness as that?"

"*Is* it foolishness, Captain?" A Sister with a face like a bird's held his eyes. "Under God's Oath, would you say it's not so?"

"That is not a proper question," growled a priest

seated next to Sister-Major. He was a heavyset man with a florid face. "You're accusing Captain Haggart, not asking him at all."

"Brother Matthew's right," chimed another. "I don't blame the Captain for what he's saying. This whole business smells more like a hanging than a hearing, and that's God's Truth!"

Suddenly, the table exploded in heated anger. Good Brothers and Sisters shook their fists at one another in a most unchurchly manner. Jeffrey turned red, and beat his fist for order to no avail. Lars was pleased and astonished at what he saw. Sister-Major was outnumbered, but certainly not alone. Of a dozen or so in the room, four at least were in her camp.

"Enough!" Jeffrey bellowed, fighting to cool the rage that mottled his flesh. "I will repeat it once more if I must. No one in this room is accusing Captain Haggart or anyone else. If there's fault or blame to be found then we'll find it. With your indulgence, Brothers and Sisters, and God's help." With a testy smile at his fellows, he turned to Lars. "Brother Job had a reason for his query; it was not simply folly to raise your ire. The question's been raised regarding the trust in your command by your own—or the lack of it, perhaps."

"That last isn't called for," Matthew warned.

"Why, then I withdraw it, of course." Jeffrey let a smile touch his lips. "Bring in the witness Amian Morse, lieutenant of the Arm of God Regiment of Mother Church."

Lars went rigid and stared in disbelief. Wherever Morse had gone, he'd never expected to find him here! A door opened, and a guard ushered Amian into the room. He met Lars' eyes a brief instant, then quickly looked away.

"If you'd care to sit, lieutenant, why you may," said Jeffrey.

"No, I'll—stand, if it's all the same," Amian muttered.

Lars glanced quickly about the table. If any save Jeffrey had been expecting this surprise, none betrayed it with their eyes.

"I wish to state clearly," said Jeffrey, "that this man came to me. I did not seek him out or ask him to come. That's true, is it not?"

"Yes, it's true."

"Speak up, please, lieutenant."

"I said it's *true!*" Morse growled.

"Fine. Proceed, then, if you will. Just tell the Board—and Captain Haggart, what you've told to me."

Morse chewed his beard and shuffled his boots. Sweat touched his brow, and he clearly wished he were anywhere else but where he was.

Amian, you poor bastard, Lars thought. *It's ever the way, is it not? Act first and think later, if you remember to think at all. . . .*

"I want to say first out," Morse muttered, "that I've nothing against Lars personal. I'm—I'm doing what I'm doing for the good of the Corps. I don't like Churchers no more'n I ever did or ever will. Far as I'm concerned you're all a bunch of pious—"

"You've made your point," Jeffrey said wearily, "get on with it, please."

"Yeah, well . . ." Amian glanced at Lars and then away. "Captain—Captain Haggart led us out there and got us killed is what he did. Those demons are hard as nails, but by God we could've done better than that. If he hadn't—"

Amian stopped short, and Lars saw the mix of tears and anger in his eyes.

"If he hadn't what?" Jeffrey prompted.

"If he'd done what we were supposed to do in the first place, a lot of good folk'd be alive!"

God's Breath, here it comes.

"And what was that, lieutenant?"

"We were—going to hit the demons on two flanks at the maze. It was all worked out. Then—right before we were set to take off, he called us to him and said we weren't goin' to do that at all, we'd do this other thing instead."

The Board looked stunned at Amian's words. Brother Job came straight up out of his chair. —As if Jeffrey had him on a string, thought Lars. "Captain Haggart *changed* his orders? In defiance of the Board and the Holy Book?"

"Yeah, I guess."

Jeffrey looked grave. "Don't *guess*, lieutenant. He either changed Sister-Major's orders or he didn't. Which is it, now?"

Amian looked at the floor. "We didn't do what we were supposed to do," he said crossly. "I just told you that, didn't I?"

"Yes, you did indeed." Jeffrey turned to Lars. "How did you dare such a thing, Captain Haggart? The Book is God's Word. Who are you to *defy* that word?"

Lars looked astonished. "Why, I didn't, of course. I followed the Word of God right to the letter."

"I warn you, Lars Haggart. Don't toy with this council!"

"I wouldn't dream of it, Brother." Lars shook his head at Morse, as if he were scolding a naughty child. "This man has a personal quarrel with me, and you know it. That's why he's here, and not to seek the truth. I *did* follow orders—in the end, at least, and that's what counts in God's eyes, does it not? I'll admit, now, I considered defying the Board, but thought better of it. My conscience got the best of me, Praise God. That's when I called my officers to me and switched *back* to God's plan—and Sister-Major's, of course."

"That's a lie!" Morse blurted.

"And how would you know?" Lars said gently. "It was me and not you that met with Sister-Major 'fore the battle. You're a good man at heart, Amian Morse. I know you're sorely troubled or you'd never say what you're saying. May God forgive your sins, for I surely do. . . ."

"Saints' Holy Blood," Jeffrey spluttered, "the man's a blasphemer as well as a liar!"

"One of the two is," Matthew pointed out. "I don't know how you can say which it is, Brother Jeffrey. I suggest we simply *ask* Sister-Major, and put an end to this. Most surely, *she* knows the orders she gave."

Every eye shifted to Sister-Major Celeste. Jeffrey watched her intently. Lars wasn't concerned, for he knew already what she'd say. She'd committed herself and wouldn't back away. A lie was a menial sin, but there was a great deal more at stake than that.

"Brother Matthew's right," Sister-Major said calmly. "We might all give pause to wonder why Good Brother Jeffrey's gone to all this trouble, when I could have given him the answer." She stood and let her iron-gray eyes sweep the room. If there was any fear about her she hid it well. "Let's get this out in the open, shall we not? I was relieved of my command after the battle, by majority vote of this Board. A vote at the insistence of Brother Jeffrey—my, ah, successor in the field, a priest and a clerk who's never commanded a flock of pigs—"

"This has nothing to do with the issue at hand," Jeffrey exploded. "A question was put to you, Sister!"

"—At the time of that vote," Sister-Major went on, "the issue seemed to be that I'd not properly guided Captain Haggart. Now, it seems, Lars Haggart stands accused of disobeying *me*. Should you not decide exactly what you're after, Brother Jeffrey? Did I obey the Board, but fail to properly interpret The Book? Did Captain Haggart obey me—and the Board and The Book as well—but fail to, ah—properly interpret my improper interpretation? Or perhaps both the Captain and myself—"

"Do you intend to answer the question or not?" Jeffrey said harshly.

"Oh, I'll answer it, for certain. As I say, you *should* have asked before now. But then we'd have missed all the dramatics, would we not?" She looked steadily about the room. "Captain Lars Haggart followed my orders to the letter." Her eyes sliced through Amian like a blade. "I fear one of the Holy Unborn in this room is guiltless—and the other is a bald-faced liar. . . ."

"*No!*" Amian Morse trembled with rage and shook an accusing finger at Lars. "Ask Lars Haggart about the Holy Unborn, why don't you? He'll t-tell you there's no such thing—that we're mortal like everyone else!"

"What's that!" Jeffrey came out of his chair, triumph already alight in his eyes.

"It's true," Morse shouted. "Him and Will Travers went to some—some *devil's* place in their dreams, where people are floatin' about. Don't say I'm a liar,

Lars, 'cause I was hiding and heard it all. You can't deny that's true!"

For an instant, deathly silence met Amian's words.

"*God's Breath*," Lars groaned, "*now you've done it, you fool. . . .*"

TWENTY

Jeffrey spread his hands for quiet, but it was a full minute or more 'fore the Board settled to any semblance of order. Lars looked past the shaking fists and angry faces to Sister-Major. Her gaunt features were frozen in disbelief; he wished there'd been a chance to get her aside, to tell her what he'd learned before the others knew it as well. How could he have guessed Morse would pull a thing like this!

"*Captain Haggart . . .*" Jeffrey stared at Lars, his face a fine study in mock horror, an expression that barely masked the flush of joy on his cheeks. "Do you answer the witness, Captain? Do you deny the charges made?"

"No," Lars said calmly, "I don't deny them at all. Your Good Brother Jerome guessed wrong. He didn't rob heaven, he merely opened a kind of door 'tween one real world and another and pulled us through. Twist it all you want—and I'm sure you will—what I've said is no reflection on Mother Church. Not if she stands for facing the truth."

"God preserve us," an elder Sister moaned.

"Amen!" shouted another.

Jeffrey made the Sign, and stalked 'round Lars like

a wolf. "God's Witness, Lars Haggart, I hope you know what you're about, for you risk your soul immortal with every word you speak!" He turned again and let his eyes sweep the others. "The demons stand howling at our gates, I don't need to tell you that. We face a greater peril than we've ever faced before. We need every blessed soldier we can get if we're not to perish. If we fail, if we falter for but a moment. . . ." His arm swung about and stabbed at Lars. "And what stands against us in this hour of our need? *Satan's spawn himself—with lies to cloud our minds and blind our eyes!*"

Lars laughed aloud. "Make up your mind, priest. I can't be God's Unborn, and Satan's spawn as well."

Jeffrey gave him a cunning smile. "And which would you say you were, Lars Haggart?"

"I know full well what I am, Good Brother. It's you that has the problem. First you ask if I deny your bloody charges, then you say it's all a lie. You can't have it forward and backward both."

Jeffrey ignored his taunts of reason. "This place of devils you saw. Tell us more of that."

"I saw nothing of the sort," Lars scoffed. "That's Amian's tale, not mine."

"But you did see *some*thing," Jeffrey persisted. "You don't deny you went to magic lands, and saw strange beings and such?"

"I saw other beings, and spoke to them as well. And none were any different than the persons about this table."

The Brothers and Sisters didn't care for that. Jeffrey picked it up at once and tossed it back. "You'd name these good folk here as fiends and imps? God's Word, how much further will you go?"

"How far will *you* go, Brother, to put words in my

mouth I never spoke!" Lars' eyes blazed with such a fury that Jeffrey stepped away. "My God, people— why would I *invent* such a tale—to raise your ire and turn you all against me? Where's the sense in that!"

"We know the reason well," snapped Jeffrey. "You'd use this lie to turn your folk 'gainst Mother Church—to keep them out of the fight!" He glanced at Morse then back to Lars. "Your own lieutenant heard your plans. How you'd leave us to fight alone and take your folk to another world. Why, you act as if the demons are your brothers, Lars Haggart. God's Word, how could you aid them any better!"

"I know a way and so do you," Lars said sharply. "Why don't you tell the Board about the Book of Armageddon, Good Brother? *Maybe they'd like to know how you plan to take us all to God's Kingdom— whether we're ready to go or not!*"

Jeffrey's face went slack. He staggered back as if Lars had dealt him a blow. Every man and woman on the Board turned white. Only a few had the presence to make the Sign.

"You—*dare* speak of this?" Jeffrey rasped. "God help us, then you're a part of that as well. I didn't know, but I should have guessed!"

"*Me!*" Lars gripped the hilt of his blade. "Oh, no, damn you—you'll not use me to worm out of this!"

"Use you, Lars Haggart?" Jeffrey's features stretched in a grin. "How could I, now, when it's you and that viper among us who's used us all?" He turned and looked directly at Sister-Major. "I'd never intended to bring this—this abomination to the Board, for it's a matter for the Holy Mother herself. Lars Haggart has left me no choice: Sister-Major Celeste of the Holy Order of Arms, I formally charge you with

173

heresy, practicing rites forbidden, and consorting with agents of Satan."

"That's a lie and you know it!" Sister-Major came to her feet, her face livid with rage. "It's you who's taken up the Devil's way, not I!"

God's Mercy, thought Lars, *he's turned the thing around and set it against us . . . he was ready for this—he's left nothing to chance to bring us down. . . .*

"Then why was this—this *filth* found in *your* quarters, Sister, and not mine?" asked Jeffrey, the gleam of victory in his eyes. "Good Sister Agatha found this concealed in your belongings—a friend who gave you her trust, as did we all." Jeffrey reached beneath his chair and tossed a heavy bound volume on the table. Brothers and Sisters gasped and shrank away, as if a serpent had suddenly appeared before their eyes. It was a thick book covered in black leather, and clearly incredibly old. Lars knew at once it could be nothing but the Book of Armageddon itself.

"Damn your soul," Sister-Major said tightly, "that's not mine and you know it!"

"It's all clear now, is it not?" Jeffrey addressed the table. "The way Sister-Major and Lars Haggart wasted the Arm of God forces in a *suicidal* attack? I'll not quote that damnable book, but what they've done's Satan's way and nothing less— Does not the Devil mock God's own commandment—give your life to gain His Kingdom? Only the kingdom you'll gain from *that's* not heaven, but hell itself!"

Brother Michael came abruptly to his feet. "That book's no evidence at all," he said bluntly. "Anyone could say a Sister found it where she did. You could have put it there yourself, and it wouldn't surprise me a bit to learn you did."

Jeffrey gave him a patient smile. "It doesn't surprise me, Good Brother, that you'd defend this traitor as you have. I've solid proof you're into this up to your neck—and you, Sister Charity and Sister Grace. And Brother Mark and Brother Andrew as well!"

Brother Michael turned pale. His bulk seemed to shrink before Lars' eyes. A sister gave a cry and brought a trembling hand to her face. Lars guessed she was one of those named.

Jeffrey turned to Lars. "Consider yourself under arrest, Captain. You'll have your chance to answer charges, but till that time you'll remain in Citadel. Lieutenant Morse, your rank is captain, now. The Arm of God Regiment is in your charge."

"Well, we can all sleep better now," Lars grinned. Amian's face colored to his hair. "You'll keep me here *how*, Brother Jeffrey? I don't think I'd find the lower reaches of Citadel much to my liking."

"No?" Jeffrey raised a quizzical brow. "Why, your friend Will Travers is there, Captain. You'd not care to speak to him?"

"Will— *What?*" A sudden chill gripped Lars Haggart's vitals. "You're lying, priest—the old man would never come here!" He knew, though, that Jeffrey meant exactly what he said. He turned and let his eyes sweep the room in desperation. "Damn me, are you *all* here in his sway? Don't you see what it is he's doing? He knows the old man can't jump— Morse had told him that. He's not a witness, for God's sake, he's a *hostage*. He's using you, me—*all* of us to further his scheme!"

Lars searched their faces, but his words met nothing but silence. A moment before, those who'd openly challenged Jeffrey had shown defiance in their eyes.

Now, Lars saw only resignation and fear, for they knew Jeffrey had nearly won the game.

"You're mistaken, Captain," Brother Job said abruptly, "if you think you'll not be treated with all fairness by this council. There's no *scheme* or cunning plot against you. If you and those accused are without sin, why you've nothing at all to fear."

Lars gave him a hollow laugh. "Somehow, I find little comfort in the words of Jeffrey's shadow."

"Nor do I," said Sister-Major.

"God's Witness, *enough!*" Jeffrey drew himself up with such a fury that even Lars, for just an instant, believed his anger was real. "We began this hearing with a question of disobedience to the Book—serious enough in nature, but it palls before the evil that's come to light." His dark eyes swept the room and stopped at Lars. "You think you're being used, Lars Haggart? Well, God's Truth, you are, but not by me. It's that woman there, our *Good* Sister-Major, who's used us all in her Devil's plan!"

An anguished cry rose from Sister-Major's throat. Her chair clattered aside as she came at Brother Jeffrey with a will. Brother Michael and another held her back. Sister-Major trembled in their grasp, and her eyes never left Brother Jeffrey.

"You see," Jeffrey crowed, "her sin's beginning to fry her rotten flesh!"

"My God," snapped Lars, "we're not *all* fools here, man."

Jeffrey shook his head. "I'll not waste time with you, Lars Haggart. There's nothing I can say you'd wish to hear."

"Now that's the first truth I've heard from your mouth today."

"You want *truth*, do you, Captain? A truth even

you, corrupt as you are, can scarce deny? Fair enough, then." Jeffrey turned slowly, and faced the Board once more. "I must tell you now there's another here among us. At her own request she's listened, and heard every word we've said. I'd ask her humbly now if she'd grace us with her presence."

Jeffrey paused, then walked to the end of the room, stopped, and gave a reverent bow. A half-open door swung wide, and a pair of Churcher guards in robes of blue helped the gaunt and fragile Sister of the Veil to a chair.

Lars sucked in a breath. Brothers and Sisters came quickly to their feet and bowed low. The Holy Virgin Mother Anne Marie walked into the room and paused.

"Blessings on you all," she said gently. "May God smile upon you." Her glance swept the table, pausing for an instant to touch every person there. When her eyes met Lars', he started and nearly fell, for it seemed as if he could feel her lips a'fresh upon his own.

"Will you sit, Holy Mother?" asked Jeffrey. "I'll have your chair brought in if you like."

"No, I think I'll stand, Jeffrey. What I have to say will take little of your time, and is better said a'standing."

Lars' mind raced. He doubted not at all this was more of Jeffrey's cunning—that somehow it was he who'd put the idea to listen in Anne Marie's head. Why, though? What did he hope to gain?

"We honor your presence here, Mother," Jeffrey said soberly. "Our hearts are heavy with this dilemma, and God's Voice is sorely needed." He glanced at Lars and Sister-Major. "You've heard, Mother, that these two stand accused of heresy and sin of the gravest degree. We beseech you to—"

"Oh, Jeffrey," Anne Marie scolded, "you don't have to go through all that. I *did* hear it, as you say." She frowned at them all and shook her head. "I'm just sure there's some mistake about that—that simply awful book, whatever it is."

"Armageddon, Mother," Brother Job prompted.

"Yes, that's the one." Anne Marie made a face. "I can tell you right now, God Himself is not at *all* pleased with this bickering and fighting. He thinks you're acting like children, and I agree. I don't for one minute believe that you, Jeffrey, or Sister-Major or Lars Haggart would have anything to do with such nonsense. Do I make myself perfectly clear?"

"If I may speak, Holy Mother—"

"That's *all*, Jeffrey," she said sternly, "all right?"

"Yes, Mother," Jeffrey said contritely.

Anne Marie looked narrowly at Lars. "And you, Lars Haggart, I cannot imagine why you've said the things you have, but I want you to know you've caused me sorrow and disappointment in the saying." Her hands went to her hips in girlish anger. "How can you dare tell such a story, that you're—*mortal*, and not one of God's Unborn? Why, Lars, would you say such a thing!"

"Mother," Lars began, "it, ah—takes some explaining but it's true. You see I—"

"It is *not* true," Anne Marie snapped. Her eyes got enormous and her chin came out in a pout. "God's Holy Voice, have you forgotten? Of course you're the Blessed Unborn—what else could you possibly be, and ravish my soul as sweetly as you did? Do you think for one minute I'd share divine carnal knowledge with a—a mortal being? What do you think I am?"

"Now just a minute—!" Lars protested.

A Good Sister shrieked and fell limply to the floor.

"God on High," moaned Brother Job, "save us from the fiend who walks among us!"

"Quiet, all of you!" Jeffrey shouted. "Sit down, please, Brothers and Sisters. It seems we have even—graver heresy a'foot than we'd imagined. . . ." His eyes blazed at Lars, and Lars could almost hear the sound of the final piece of the puzzle click into place.

TWENTY-ONE

"Damn it all, Lars, I won't have you doin' this," Will grumbled. "Get yourself out of here and don't bother 'bout me."

"Let's hear no more about it," Lars said firmly. "When I leave, Will, we'll all leave."

"And just how you figure on doing that?"

"If I *knew* how then I'd do it, all right?"

"I shouldn't have let it happen. It was a damn fool thing to do."

"Forget about it, Will."

"They came for you and I didn't even think. Sean told 'em you were gone, and 'fore I knew it they'd knocked him flat and had me down. Wasn't anything I could do."

"Stop blaming yourself. They had it all figured out."

"If I was a few years younger I'd have shown 'em."

"God's Eyes," Lars snapped, "shut up and let me think!"

Will Travers muttered to himself and stalked away. He moved but a few short meters before the wall of the cell came to an end. The guards beyond the bars watched him intently. When Will moved, the blunt curve of their crossbows moved with him. Lars knew he could jump and take the first before he could ever loose a bolt. There was no way on earth he could get them both. He knew it, and the Churchers knew it as well.

Lars turned and walked to the far corner of the cell. Sister-Major hadn't moved for the past half hour. She stood stiff as a rod and glared at the wall.

"You're just going to stand there, are you? We have to talk, you know."

"I've nothing to say to you, Captain. I thought I made that clear."

"You did, but it's not good enough. You don't have to like me, Sister-Major, but you do have to admit that we share a common problem. Good Brother Jeffrey wants to see us both dead. To me, that's reason enough to talk."

Sister-Major turned abruptly. "All right, Lars Haggart—talk. But God's Witness, I'll tell you plain again—"

"I know," Lars said wearily, "if we get through this you'll kill me yourself. And I'm telling *you* again, damn it— I did *not ravish* the Holy Mother. God's Blood, the poor lass doesn't even know what it means. *Lust* and *carnal knowledge* are words she plucked out of a book. I'll grant she's ah—got the urges and desires a young girl's bound to feel, but she's no idea what they're for. . . ."

"Stop!" Sister-Major slapped her hands to her ears. "Praise God, don't tell me any more!"

"Fine," Lars said bluntly, "let's talk on lovely matters that won't offend your saintly self—like intrigue and whispers and secrets of the court. How did Jeffrey know I was there with Holy Mother, tell me that? It may be Ham betrayed me but I doubt it."

"He wouldn't have to," she said. "Holy Mother has folk who run about and see to her needs. One of them, I'd guess, belongs in Jeffrey's camp."

"Or knows someone who is."

"We underestimated the man, and now we're paying the price. I blame myself for that."

"What'll happen to her now? Would Jeffrey do her harm?"

Sister-Major looked appalled. "Of course he'll do her no harm. The Holy Mother's God's Voice. Even Jeffrey wouldn't think of such a thing!"

"Ah, fine," Lars said dryly. "Then all's well, is it not? I'm one of God's Unborn, and all that happened to Will and me was only a dream. I did indeed divinely ravish Holy Mother, for that's what she says I did. And of course we don't need to worry 'bout Armageddon. Herself said very clearly we must put such foolishness aside. Damn me, Sister—I don't see why we need to leave this cell."

Sister-Major gave him a quick and cutting look. "It's neither your place nor mine to question God's plan, Lars Haggart. If the way seems somewhat— muddled and at odds, then I'd guess God is testing our faith. . . ."

"He's certainly testing mine," muttered Lars. He peered past her shoulder at the guards. "If I could get those two to turn away for just a bit, or even one, mind you— *Saints, what's that!*"

Suddenly, a terrible clamor broke the silence. The guards stood straight and stared. From the level above came muted shouts of alarm, and the thunder of heavy boots.

"Demons," Sister-Major gasped. "God help us, they're attacking Citadel!"

"Is that possible? Could they be as close as that?"

Before she could answer, something hard and heavy hit the stone wall above. An awesome sound shuddered the Keep, a blow so strong Lars could feel it in his boots.

"Damn me, what's that?" said Will. He came to Lars' side, dodging drifts of dust from the ceiling. The sound came again, a steady and thunderous rhythm.

"A ram," Sister-Major said sharply. "Someone's trying to knock down the walls. . . ."

"And doing a fair job, too."

A heavy door burst open down the hall. One of the guards jerked about and aimed his weapon.

"Lower that, soldier!" a voice said harshly.

"Uh—yes, *sir!* Sorry, sir!" The guard snapped to attention, and turned back to his business. A burly Churcher captain marched quickly down the hall. Six men followed, all in helms and heavy armor. Without breaking stride, the first two troopers brought their fists down hard on the guards' cocked weapons. Iron-headed bolts sparked the floor. The startled guards cried out as troopers wrestled them to the ground. Two well-placed blows, and the pair went silent. Someone produced a key from the guardsman's belt. Seconds later the cell was open.

"Sister-Major Celeste. . . ." The captain raised his helm, shot her an anxious salute and stepped forward. "Are you all right, ma'am?"

"I am now," she smiled, "and pleased to see you, Captain Micah. I don't know how you found us, but I'm grateful that you did."

Captain Micah cleared his throat. "I can't take credit, Sister-Major. The corporal here did that. He's not one of ours, but he said you needed help."

"Ham!" Lars spotted the black-agate eyes and

rodent beak. "Saints, if you're not a sight for sore eyes!"

Ham grinned shyly, and saluted Sister-Major. "Your service, ma'am. Lars Haggart and me are close as twins. Just ask him and he'll tell you."

"I'll not hold you to blame for that," she said darkly. "Micah, the situation and quickly. How the devil did the demons break through? Can we hold them back or not?"

Micah flushed. "It's—not the demons, ma'am. Leastways not as yet. It's the townsfolk—old men and grannies, and every farmer who's got a sharp stick or a fork."

"What!"

"God's Truth, Sister. They tore up everything in sight, and now they're after Citadel."

"Let me guess," Lars said dryly. "Someone spread the word Holy Mother's been—what? Possessed by the devil himself? Lars Haggart, and his crew of fiery imps. And of course Good Sister-Major, the daughter of evil herself. . . ."

Micah looked astonished. "How did you know that?"

"I didn't. I know Brother Jeffrey."

"*Damn* that fool!" Sister-Major's face went taut with rage. "He's madder than I guessed. Micah, who can we trust? How many of the regiments will follow me?"

Micah squirmed uncomfortably. "Ma'am, they're all scared out of their wits. Brother-Major Jeffrey's got the Third and the Fifteenth, I know that."

"And both of those at the front," Sister-Major said to herself. "Which means he's only got the Keep Guards to hold the townsmen. I can count on the Fourth and Twenty-Third, and likely the Seventh and another. Fighting our own folk. That's what he's brought us to!" She turned to face them all. "Quickly, we've no more business down here, and I don't like the sound of walls coming down around my neck."

She led them down the hall and up the narrow stone stairs. The ram had gone silent, but the swell of angry voices was ever louder. Micah told her he had more troopers ahead, hiding in a storeroom under the kitchens. Sister-Major sent a sergeant on ahead. Before another minute passed he was back, tension straining his features.

"They've found us," he blurted. "Lieutenant Aaron's dead. Sergeant Gideon's taken over. The whole Keep Guard's out there and they've cut us off. Gideon's retreating back here as best he can."

"Tell Gideon to hold," Micah said sharply. "There's no way *out* but the way we came!" The sergeant snapped a quick salute and headed off.

"Can we hold them?" Lars asked anxiously. "I can jump and get help, if you'll tell me where to go."

Sister-Major shook her head. "Who's going to trust Lars Haggart? Damn me, I'm not even sure where I'd send you if I could." She turned and stared thoughtfully at Micah. "You're wrong, Captain. There is another way out of the lower levels."

Micah looked surprised. "You're certain, Sister-Major?"

"This is the oldest part of Citadel, built just after The Landing. There's a way back up—but it goes through sacred ground."

"Well, let's not worry about that," said Lars.

"You don't understand. When the ship that brought our ancestors was forced to land, they buried it under the Keep. We'll have to pass through the ship to get up to Citadel."

Micah and Ham went pale. "Do we dare such a

thing?" asked the captain. "Your pardon, Sister-Major, but I'd just as soon face Jeffrey's men as shades of the past!"

Sister-Major gave him a look. "Tell your men to fall back in good order, Captain Micah. Quickly, now, or we'll all be shades soon enough."

Before Sister-Major reached the next bend in the tunnel, the sound of Micah's action met their ears. She raised her torch and led them hurriedly down one twisted way and then another.

"Our folk at the barracks," asked Will when he had the chance, "do you know what's happened to them?"

Ham made a face. "I know the mob went for 'em first, when the ugly talk 'bout Holy Mother got started. Don't guess that surprises you much."

"They'll scatter," said Will. "Sean and Carilee know what to do."

"If your friend *Captain* Morse hasn't got them," Sister-Major said darkly.

Lars shook his head. "Jeffrey erred in that. He used Morse badly, but that's the end of it."

Will Travers gave a bitter little laugh. "Put your mind at ease, Sister. Starvin' dogs wouldn't follow Amian Morse to a feast."

The tunnel ahead narrowed and came to an end. Sister-Major stopped, and swept her torch about. The ancient stonework glistened with beaded moisture. In the center of the wall, the rock was cut away to bare a large metal circle near two full meters about. The metal was dull as pewter, but neither scarred nor rusted with age.

"Saints keep us," Ham whispered, "I'd rather die right here th-than go a step farther. . . ."

"Corporal, that's exactly the choice you've got," said Sister-Major. "Now stop your foolish shaking and get Micah and the others here fast. Hurry, now, or God's my judge, I'll make you go in first."

TWENTY-TWO

Ham scampered off, clearly glad to be gone. The four other troopers kept their distance, hoping Sister-Major wouldn't notice they were there.

"Hold this light, Lars Haggart, and I'll try to make us a way. Pray God I can remember how it's done."

She bent to a groove in the ancient metal Lars hadn't noticed before. Shouts and cries of alarm sounded behind, closer than ever now. Ham's companions hefted their weapons and formed a shield at their leader's back.

Lars heard a slight whisper of sound. Sister-Major stepped back. The circle sprang clear a good inch. Slipping her fingers around the edge, she pushed the portal aside with no effort.

"It works like a marvel," said Lars. "And after all this time!"

"They were a different kind of folk," said Sister-Major. "Past our understanding, for certain."

"And is this perhaps where the Good Brother Jerome found his magic?"

Sister-Major's eyes went flat. "Brother Jerome is no concern of yours, Lars Haggart."

"Oh, no? If not for him I'd be dancing by a river

with lovely maids, 'stead of mucking about in some cellar."

"You—don't know what you're saying," she snapped. "You're God's Unborn, and I strongly doubt he'd have you cavorting with maids and such!"

Before Lars could answer, a shout went up behind him. A squad of Micah's troops burst 'round the corner, turned and went to their knees and loosed their bolts. A thick flurry of arrows hummed past, snapping their shafts against stone. A soldier threw up his weapon and cried out, a feathered tail between his ribs. In an instant, a steady stream of troopers filled the tunnel. Micah shouted them on, and Sister-Major hurried them into the ship. Nearly all showed the blood of fierce encounter. They were hollow-eyed with shock, too concerned with the foe behind to greatly care what lay ahead.

Micah waited till the last man was through, then shouted his rearguard to the ship.

"All right, shut it!" yelled Lars.

"Wait, one thing more," said Sister-Major. She slipped past Lars, the burnt stub of a torch in her fist.

"Damn it, Sister, get back in here!"

Jeffrey's Guardsmen turned the corner, saw the open door and gave a shout. Arrows and lances sparked stone. Sister-Major calmly went to her knees and scratched at the floor. Lars cursed, grabbed her up bodily and carried her into the ship. Will and Micah slammed the door. A volley of missles rattled harmlessly off metal.

Sister-Major pushed Lars angrily away. "Don't you—*ever* do that," she warned. "I'll not have you touch me, Lars Haggart!"

"Fine. Don't do something ridiculous and I won't."

"That *ridiculous* thing I did will very likely save your hide. I drew a skull and cross upon the floor. It's the ancient sign of death, and they'll think twice again 'fore they pass it."

Lars shot her a dubious look. "Can anyone else open that lock?"

"No one who'll come down here. You must know the right numbers to set it free."

Lars turned to Ham. "Get a few blades, jam 'em in that lock and break them off."

Sister-Major sighed. "You've no faith in God, Lars Haggart."

"That's not *God* out there who wants our hides," Lars told her.

If Lars expected ancient wonders he was sadly disappointed. The vessel was a vast, enormous shell, a dark and empty cavern and nothing more. Whatever marvels there'd been to see had long vanished. Now and then he caught a shadow along the great concavity of the hull; a square of metal or a circle, a hint of something abruptly sheered away. When he followed this curve with his eyes he saw a pattern, and guessed immense ribbing had formed the sturdy bones of the ship. He could scarce imagine how big the vessel might be, for darkness drank the feeble light of their torches.

"What happened here?" he asked Sister-Major in a whisper. It seemed to Lars the proper voice for such a place. "I know it didn't look like this in the beginning."

"No, not like this at all. There were walls and ceilings and endless rooms, wondrous machines and magic lights. Through the years, we've taken everything we could to lighten our burden. All the metal on Harmony comes from here. The stuff of plows and nails and lances. There's no more sacred place than this."

What's left of it, thought Lars. "And what made the vessel go? Move from one world to another?"

"God, of course. What kind of fool question is that?"

"He, ah—just pulled it along like a wagon, then, did he?"

" 'He caused great fire to shoot forth,' " Sister-Major quoted. " 'Like unto a comet 'cross the Heavens.' "

"Fire pulled the vessel?"

"Pushed," Sister-Major corrected. "There's a firing room in the rear of the ship. They say He Himself was seen there at times. I went in once when I was young, during the reign of the last Holy Mother. It was empty, of course, but—"

"But what?"

"Damn me," she said crossly, "why am I telling *you* all this? Here, take the torch awhile. Make yourself useful if you can." She grasped the heavy folds of her robes and waded through a shallow pool. Farther along they passed a spot where a cold veil of water rained continuously onto the way. Lars waited, holding his torch high while Micah's men crossed to drier ground.

"I don't like this place," said Ham, his eyes black as oil in the fading light. "It's not a seemly place to be, Lars Haggart."

"It's somewhat *seemlier* than an arrow in the belly," said Lars.

"Be that as it may, I could use a swallow of good corn ale right now. God's Truth I could."

"Ham," Lars said plainly, "were you still outside, when the Churchers came charging up the stairs?"

Ham looked right at him. "I didn't betray you, friend. I didn't even know who you met and still don't. I'm sorry you have to ask."

"Damn it all, I *know* you didn't, Ham. I never thought you did," Lars lied. "I was only wondering if you'd know who it was."

"Now *that* I can answer," he said, granting Lars a wily grin. "A sergeant in the Holy Order Guards. A fellow I thought I could trust." He ran a finger quickly across his throat. "He's a true friend, now—there's no more trustworthy fellow about."

Lars didn't doubt it for a moment. He turned to look for Will, and saw him far ahead.

"Micah—Captain Haggart! Hurry along and bring more light!" Lars and Ham joined Micah, and three other troopers with torches. Sister-Major stood by the wall, impatiently stamping her foot. A section of metal had been removed long ago, revealing stone steps that vanished into the dark.

"We climb up past the ship, and into Citadel," she explained. "If I remember right, this leads to a second-floor chamber. Micah, the way's hard. Put your best up front. How many able-bodied do you count?"

"Twenty, twenty-five," Micah said grimly. "We lost a good half of what we had."

"They're with God, then, and better off than you or I." She made the Sign and looked at Lars. "Lead the way if you will, Captain Haggart. God's Heart is with us, and he means to win this day!"

"Fine," said Lars, "that's a blessed relief to know."

Long before he reached the top he could hear it, the strident ring of iron against iron, the anguished cries of warring men. Passing the torch behind him, he took the last steps in gloomy dark.

"There's wood here," he said softly, "some kind of a panel."

"Run your hand to the right," said Sister-Major. "There'll be a bolt of sorts. Slide it back gently. Take a careful look before you commit us."

"Thank you. The thought had occurred to me."

The bolt was where she'd said, and opened without a sound. Lars peeked into a room full of stout wooden shelves and narrow aisles. The shelves were stuffed to the ceiling with dusty rolls of parchment. There was a door at the far end of the room. It sounded to Lars as if a battle were in full swing behind it. Squeezing past the panel, he made his way quickly through the shelving and eased the bolt shut across the door. He let out a breath and turned about as the others filled the room.

Sister-Major looked pleased. "Just as I remembered. It's the library, second level of the Keep."

"I wonder who's doing all the shouting, theirs or ours?"

"Sister-Major," called Micah, "over here please, quickly!" Lars followed, and Micah looked grimly at them both. "Out there. You'd best see for yourself." Micah's men had pushed heavy shelving aside to reveal a narrow window. Past it was a closed sentry-walk and a low stone battlement. The sound of heavy fighting came from below. Lars crawled to a stone embrasure and looked down.

"Holy God," he said under his breath. The sight near set him on his heels. Hordes of angry townsmen had crossed the bridge and breached the outer wall. It was the sound of their heavy ram he'd heard from below. From the carnage past the wall, it was clear they'd fought a fierce and bloody battle with Jeffrey's men. Now, swelled with ever-growing numbers, they swarmed the narrow bailey, the inner courtyard of the Keep, and into the Citadel itself.

"Damn you, Jeffrey," Sister-Major said tightly, "you've loosed the devil sure, and we'll pay bloody coin 'fore we get him back in his cage!"

As Lars watched, the townsmen surged forward, wicked scythes and forks pressing the Guardsmen steadily back. The soldiers did their best, but the townsmen rolled over them by the hundreds.

"Any ideas?" asked Lars. "That racket outside our door is Jeffrey's folk. If they can't stand firm. . . ."

"They can't." Sister-Major shook her head. "A few minutes more and that's it. Micah! Get a squad out of the Keep. The northern front's too far, and we dare not pull a man from there. Get through to the south. Isaiah and Malachi will follow me. We *must* get men to Citadel!"

Micah frowned. "Begging your pardon, Sister. . . . What do we do *then?* Fight Jeffrey's folk or the townsmen?"

"Use your head," she said sharply. "We bring back order, whatever that takes. Now get your men and go." Sister-Major turned to Lars. "A small squad will make it 'cross the roofs and down the Keep. We've a problem of our own to face now. God's Patience, I've twenty good men trapped in a—in a *library!*"

"Lars—" Will came quickly to his side. "Townsmen, comin' up the other side. Look there!" He pointed, and Lars and Sister-Major followed his glance. A narrow stone stairway wound about the far side of the tower. A band of townsmen had circled the fight, and were making their way stealthily up the Keep.

"If they get up there they'll have the roof and a

way inside," said Sister-Major. "Once inside, they'll have the Keep *and* Citadel."

"You can't get men over there," said Will. "They'd have to climb straight up."

Lars backed off and shaded his eyes. Directly above, a file of townsmen swarmed the crenelated battlement, only a story below the top of the Keep. Their leader paused and glanced about, a nastily curved sickle in his fist. Suddenly, he turned and pointed excitedly to his right, gave a shout and ran. The men behind him followed on his heels. At once, Lars heard a high, piercing scream that chilled his blood. His eye caught the flash of a slender figure running past the sentry-walk. Black robes billowed beneath a cap of raven hair; a face turned to bare honeyed skin and enormous frightened eyes.

"Saint's Blood," Lars gasped, "it's her—they're after Holy Mother!"

"They won't touch her," Sister-Major snapped. "They wouldn't dare!"

Lars didn't deign to answer. Clasping the hilt of his sword, he jumped. . . .

TWENTY-THREE

The burly townsman paled as Lars Haggart suddenly appeared in his path. To his credit, he found his wits and struck quickly. Lars caught the curve of the sickle in his blade and sent it flying. The townsman stumbled back. Lars stepped forward, turned his blade and tapped the fellow lightly with his pommel. The man went down with a grunt. Lars leaped past him and met the next. He was a wiry oldster with a scar that split his face, and a wooden fork for a weapon. He thrust the thing at Lars, and Lars moved lazily aside. The fork ripped his jerkin and scraped flesh. Lars yelped, cursed his lack of caution and hewed the weapon in half. Without a blink the man was on him, flailing the severed handle like a club.

"All right, damn you," Lars muttered, "enough's enough." He caught the fellow hard with the flat of his blade, and winced as he heard bone crack. He'd no wish to harm the surly bastards if he could help it. Clearly, they didn't feel the same about him.

Lars took the next pair quickly, savagely spitting one and booting the other off the wall. Another came at him and then another. They were spilling over the battlement like lice on a beggar's collar. Lars was suddenly uncomfortable with the odds. He jumped, caught the next in line unaware and split his skull. The fellow behind him retched. Lars kicked him in the belly and raced to the edge of the wall. A face appeared, and Lars kicked it soundly. The man screamed with fright and fell back, taking three companions with him. Lars peered cautiously over the edge. His last assault had slowed them down, but not for long. Someone saw him and shouted. A pair of bowmen let their arrows fly. One struck stone and the other near parted his hair. Lars ducked, and sprinted back along the sentry-walk.

Anne Marie was pressed fearfully against the wall. "We'll be all right," he assured her. "If we can get around the Keep, I can hold 'em till we get a bit of help."

"*No!*" The girl shrank back, her eyes full of fury. "You had no cause to murder those men, Lars Haggart. They—they love me dearly. They had no intention of bringing me harm."

"Right," Lars said dryly. "That's why you screamed and ran like a rabbit. Mother, we don't have time for theology at the moment. If we stand here talking we're dead."

Anne Marie protested and dug in her heels. Lars grasped her hand firmly and pulled her along. Past a high curtain wall and beneath a heavy timber hoard, he led them quickly around the Keep. The sentry-walk ended abruptly. Lars craned his neck and looked up. Just past the point where the crenelated wall met the tower, stubby butts of timber extended from stone. Following them with his eyes, he saw they led a good eight meters to the top of the Keep itself.

"Oh, no you don't!" Anne Marie guessed his

thoughts and backed off. "I'm—not going up that, Lars Haggart. I'm terrified of heights."

"Mother, would God let you fall?"

"Don't be ridiculous."

"Then you've nothing at all to fear." Before the girl could protest, he clutched her slender waist and lifted her bodily over the wall. Anne Marie shrieked and kicked. Lars winced, but stubbornly kept his grip. Suddenly, she found a hold and jerked free. Lars watched in wonder as she scrambled up the side. For a lass afraid of heights, she did a fair imitation of a lizard.

A shout brought him around. The angry horde of townsmen were hot on his heels. Lars jumped to the top of the Keep, in time to help the girl over the side.

"Don't *touch* me," she glared, brushing dark hair out of her eyes. "I don't ever wish to speak to you again, Lars Haggart!"

Lars ignored her. Sweeping his glance about the circular top of the Keep, he found what he was seeking. Extruding from the paved stone flooring was a wooden trap door. Two angles of iron were embedded in rock on either side. Lying handily nearby was a stout length of timber. Lars dragged it to the door, and kicked it under the angles.

"There." He grinned. "Satan himself couldn't get through that."

"Which means we're *stuck* up here forever."

"That's beside the point. Shut up and stop complaining." He stalked to the edge again and looked down. "Damn fools," he said under his breath. "They don't have the wits of a pig."

"What do you see?"

"More of the faithful, Mother, climbing the wall you just mounted. Coming to pay homage, no doubt."

"Don't blaspheme," she scolded. "It's you they're after, not me."

"It's me they're after 'cause of *you*," Lars said darkly. "If you had the brains of a— *God's breath, what's that!*"

Lars forgot the townsmen below and stared at the far horizon. For an instant, he was certain his eyes had deceived him. To the north, the plains and rolling hills were a'swarm with moving figures. One dark column after another was advancing on the run toward Citadel.

"What? Oh, no!" Anne Marie gasped and made the Sign. "It's the demons, they've broken through our lines!"

"We're lucky if we've *got* any lines. Its's not the demons at all, it's your own Churcher troops. Jeffrey's panicked and called them back to save his hide."

"No. . . ." Anne Marie shook her head. "He wouldn't do that. . . ."

"He would and he has, damn it." Lars grasped her shoulders hard. "It's time you grew up, Mother, and came to your senses. It's not the demons now, but you can expect 'em soon enough. I doubt it's the way Jeffrey planned it, but it'll, by God, work just as well. He's got his Armageddon for sure!"

"That's not so, Lars Haggart!" She stomped her foot and glared. "Just because you don't happen to *like* Brother Jeffrey doesn't mean you have to say such—*awful* things about him. God says we're to forgive, and love one another. I'm certain Jeffrey forgives you, and I fully expect you to do the same."

Lars looked at her. Her cheeks were flush with color, full lips moist and ripe as berries. He'd never seen a lovelier face, deeper, more breathtaking eyes. And yet, for all of that. . . . "Look," he told her, "if this works out all right, someone's got to talk to you. Maybe I'm not the one to do it. But all this business about lust and—and divine carnal sin you've got in your head—"

"—was absolutely marvelous, Lars. I can't wait to get ravished again!" Her youthful smile faded to a pout. "Which doesn't *mean* I'm not angry with you still. But I *will* forgive you, I'm certain of that."

Lars ground his teeth. "Holy Mother, listen—"

Howls of surprise and anger welled up from below. Lars left the girl and leaned to the wall. Sister-Major's soldiers were sweeping the sentry-walk, spilling one townsman after the other over the side. An instant later, the woman herself appeared, sheathed her heavy blade and started climbing in Lars' direction. Will, Ham and Micah's men followed quickly.

Sister-Major caught her breath and bowed to Anne Marie. "Holy Mother," she said anxiously, "I pray you're all right?"

"Of course," Anne Marie said sweetly. "God guards me well as ever."

Sister-Major turned to Lars. "You saw them, I imagine. That fool's talked two full regiments off the front—which means there's only four holding the line. Get to Micah to the south. He's likely reached there now. Tell him my orders are changed. He's to *leave* Malachai's regiment where it is. We can't leave the south that open. Tell him to bring only *half* Isaiah's best—and Isaiah himself. Nothing more."

"What good'll that do? Half a regiment won't hold 'gainst Jeffrey's two."

"God's Eyes," Sister-Major said crossly, "I don't want to *fight* 'em, I want to bring them over—send them back before it's too late. Isaiah's the finest we've got. The men respect him and he's with me.

He knows Jeffrey, and what he's about. The northern regiments will listen."

"If they stop long enough," said Lars.

Sister-Major gripped his arm, a gesture so unexpected it caught him totally by surprise. "Listen to me, Lars Haggart— Jeffrey's warped those men with lies, same as he has the townsmen, or they'd never turn from demons. They're frightened—they think there's a greater evil here. Isaiah's got to help me convince them they're wrong."

"That greater evil bein' me," Lars said tightly. He caught her eye. "What I told you down below's true. About Holy Mother. I don't know if it matters anymore, but I'd like for you to believe me."

Sister-Major showed no expression at all. "Like you say, right now it doesn't matter what I believe, now does it? Get out of here if you're going, Lars Haggart."

Lars swallowed his anger and turned away. At the far side of the Keep, he strained his eyes to the south. He'd never been there and didn't know the land. There was a hill on the far horizon, crowned by a thick grove of trees. He looked at the trees and jumped . . .

There was nothing past the trees but a valley, and beyond it, another hill. Lars jumped again. The Churcher armies were just below and to the east. Lars spotted a group of officers, Captain Micah among them.

The Churchers scattered in alarm and drew their blades. Micah waved them back and walked to Lars. Lars gave his message quickly, and told him about the defections in the north.

Micah paled at the news. "She's right. Isaiah could turn them if we could get him there in time. It's too far. They'll reach Citadel long before we do."

"You've got to try. You can't stop, Micah."

"Damn me, of course we'll try. What else can we do? Titus, Lieutenant Zachariah—get over here now!"

Two men broke from the officers' circle and sprinted for Lars and Micah. Suddenly, a shout went up from the ranks that stopped them in their tracks. The shout became a great cry of alarm that swept the army like a wind.

"Demons . . . demons to the rear . . . !"

Micah turned to Lars. "That's it, it's all over. Tell her we'll hold as best we can."

Lars gripped his shoulder. "Luck, Micah."

The Churcher Captain laughed. "Luck's what I'll get in heaven, Lars Haggart. And soon enough at that."

Lars jumped.

She heard the explosion of air and turned to face him. He told her quickly what had happened.

"Micah's right. God help us, we're likely finished for certain."

Lars let out a breath. "There must be someone. An officer in one of Jeffrey's regiments. I'll find him, take a message from you."

Sound welled up from the fighting below. From the Keep, they could see the first banners of the rebels to the north. The troopers were less than half a league away from Citadel. The townsmen saw them now, and panic filled their ranks. Those who'd reached the lower stories turned and fled, fighting through their fellows to the rear. The hapless townsmen massed outside ran *toward* the Keep and met them. In an instant, they were clawing at one another in mindless fear.

"They likely won't listen but you can try," said Sister-Major. "Find Brother-Captain Asshur, or Sister-

Lieutenant Naomi. They're both with the Fourth and loyal to me. Look for a red and blue banner." She peered at the rapidly advancing troops. "Hurry, at least it's worth a chance."

"Luck," said Lars, and jumped. . . .

He was well to the flank of the army's path, out of sight past a squat line of hovels that ringed the town. He had no wish to draw attention. Jeffrey'd spread the same awesome lie to rebel troopers that had turned docile townsmen into an angry, vicious mob. *Lars Haggart's Satan's own . . . the devil's soiled the Virgin Mother!*

Peering around a corner he saw them coming, grim-faced men in helm and armor on the run to Citadel. His eyes swept a sea of ragged banners. There were too many, he'd never find the one he wanted. And even if he could—

A sudden thought struck him. Maybe Sister-Major was wrong. If the Fourth had officers she could trust, maybe the regiment was still at the front. Maybe it wasn't here at all.

Lars jumped again . . .

Two leagues, three, and then another.

The awful sounds and sights of battle hit him like a storm. Iron met iron as men and demons screamed and died. The Churchers left to hold the line fought bravely, but the demons were well aware their numbers were lessened. Lars saw it, knew the instant it happened. The demons surged forward, a swarm of flesh and iron, broke the Churchers' backs and sent them fleeing. Now, the impish forces had them, panicked armies between them, driving north and south for Citadel. . . .

TWENTY-FOUR

Lars stalked the empty barracks, sword gripped loosely at his side. As Ham reported, they'd gone through the place like a storm. There was scarce a bench or chair left standing. Broken pots and dishes snapped beneath his boots. The waning day made unfamiliar shadows, turning every corner into a foe. Climbing the loft he found it empty, and the kitchen below as well. It was the same in every structure—his folk had left quickly, jumped to save their lives. And where are they now, he wondered. Had any been fool enough to follow Amian Morse?

"Captain Haggart. . . ."

He turned swiftly, bringing his blade to bear. The boy walked out of shadow and Lars relaxed. "Young MacLee—it's good to see a friendly face. The others are safe, I take it?"

"Yes, sir," MacLee nodded. "Me or someone else has been jumping back here. We knew you'd come when you could. Captain, we were worried and that's the truth. Nobody knew if you'd—"

"No, and neither did I, MacLee. Let's be off, lad. Where to?"

"The grove above the steam past Joshua's Road. A

good two leagues to the west. Carilee—*Sergeant* O'Farr—said you'd remember."

Lars did. It was a place they'd shared in happier days. He took a last look at the empty room. The barracks already smelled of dust. Stopping to listen, he could hear the sound of fighting past the town. Troopers 'gainst townsmen, or troopers 'gainst their own? Or God help us, demons against them all by now. He shook his head and jumped. . . .

The first thing Carilee said was she was glad to see him safe. Second, that if there'd been any *ravishing* going on she couldn't personally recall, he'd wish himself dead a hundred times again. Lastly, she told him Morse was gone.

"Gone where?" Lars demanded. "Back to Good Brother Jeffrey, no doubt?"

"No, Lars," Sean said soberly. "He—came back to the barracks full of bluster—how he'd managed to save you and Will from Jeffrey's wrath. Said *he* was Captain now, and was willing to lead us to safety."

"My *God*," breathed Lars.

"That didn't last. You know Morse—his thoughts got tangled and he started telling the truth. When it all came out I could have skewered him on the spot. Instead, the bloody townsmen started spilling over the walls and we'd other things to do."

"So where's the fool now?"

Carilee looked at the ground. "That's the rest of it, Lars. Sean and I led a patrol up north—not half an hour ago, just before you found us. Just a small party, we—figured we'd best know what was about for the good of us all. God, Lars, it was awful! We saw some of the Churchers pull back and start south. Of course we couldn't guess why until now. And then—after that, the demons attacked. They just—slashed right through the lines. Nobody could stop them." Carilee closed her eyes to shut out the sight.

"That's when Morse showed up," Sean finished. "I didn't even know if he'd jumped from the barracks, but there he was. We were a good half league from the front and well hidden, but the jumpers found us all the same. Four of 'em—they were suddenly just *there*. Morse came past me, bellowing like a bear and threw himself at them. I saw him cut one down in a wink. The bastard was so surprised he didn't jump." Sean paused, and looked squarely at Lars. "I know what he did before, and there's no excusing that. But he saved our hides out there, Lars. Gave us the second we needed to get away. He jumped and so did the demons and—that's the last we saw."

"Damn it all," cursed Lars, "damn *him* for being what he was. Thinking was the man's only fault. If he'd stayed himself from that. . . . I won't mind saying it, I liked the fool, whatever he did."

"There's more to what we saw," said Sean. "I think it's best you hear. The jumpers have gone wild; there's no stopping them at all. Near as I can tell, there simply *aren't* any regular jumpers now. There'll *all* longjumpers, every blessed one. I don't think it mattered whether Jeffrey's rebel troopers left or not. . . ."

Lars stared at them both. "Why, though? Why would they gain new power *now* and not before?" Suddenly, he remembered Sister-Major's words. Something was happening to the jumpers . . . they were changing. . . . How in hell had she stumbled on that?

Carilee guessed his thoughts. "You think it's over, don't you? You don't think they stand a chance."

"No, Carilee. Not a bloody chance."

"And where does that leave us?"

Lars glanced from one to the other then past them. There were a hundred of his own within the grove, all of the Corps that was left. "What do they think? What do they say?"

"They know what we're facing," said Sean. "But they don't want to run anymore. There's no love lost 'tween us and the Churchers, but they figure we're all in this together. Damn it, we can't just hide in a hole and watch."

"No," said Lars, "I don't think we can."

Lars jumped to the top of the Keep, Carilee and Sean a second behind. A trooper jerked about and then another, weapons at the ready.

"Hold, damn you!" Micah stepped forward and grasped his hand. "They're jumpy, as you might imagine. Are there any more coming?"

"Not yet. There will be. I trust you'll spread the word."

Micah nodded. Lars suddenly realized they were both nearly shouting. The din from below was a horror, the nightmare sounds of battle and dying men. Lars stepped to the battlement and looked down. For nearly a quarter-league, the ground was a mass of men and armor. Every Churcher who'd reached home safe was down below—a thousand, five thousand, ten. There were no loyal soldiers or rebels now, only men—their only allegiance life, their goal one breath and then another.

The army's outer edge was ringed with great ballistae and trebuchets, and other engines of war. Beyond that, timbers meant for a maze had been hastily butted to earth, pointed ends set at killing angles.

Past the outer ring for a good fifty meters there was nothing. And past that was a sight that set Lars' hair on end. There, the ground was a'swarm with demons, twice and three times more than the number they faced, terrible legions stretching as far as the eye could see. The imps howled and beat upon their shields, and stabbed blood pennons at the sky.

"God and Satan met in one last battle—Armageddon! Armageddon!"

"What's that?" asked Micah.

"Nothing," Lars told him. "You've had no jumpers, none at all?"

"Don't rush them. They'll be here soon enough. They're likely waiting for dark."

Lars had already delivered the bad news—that they could look for more longjumpers than they ever cared to see.

"I'm glad you made it, Micah. I didn't expect to see you again."

"No one's more surprised than me," Micah answered. "Come now, get your friends. Sister-Major will want to see you."

Sister-Major Celeste looked weary and ready to drop. Lars, though, knew the demons would have to chop her off at the knees to bring her to ground.

"You'd do that, then?" she asked intently, "that's your decision, Lars Haggart?"

"Not mine," Lars corrected. "The Karma Corps decided on their own. Sean will go back and bring them here. We're not as good as demons but we can fight. That's what we want to do."

"Fight next to Churchers."

"Yes, damn me, fight next to Churchers."

Sister-Major let a smile crack her face. "You're

welcome, then, and we're proud to have you. Though I think you're a fool," she added sharply. "What's the good of dying here, Lars Haggart? Fight you may, but you can't change the end. Not against what's waiting out there."

"We're not dead yet."

"No, we're not, Praise God." She glanced past him into the growing dark. The stub of a candle between them did little to light the room. "Micah showed you? You saw what we're doing, I guess."

"He did. I think it ought to help."

"It better. Especially in the light of what you've said." She raised a brow at Lars. "Would *you* want to jump in Citadel?"

"Not the way you've rigged it. Too bloody risky." He'd seen some of Sister-Major's work on his climb down from the roof. Every chamber and hall was being set with angles of timber, the frames then pricked with heads of lances, hooks and cutting blades. "You know they're not going to jump and find a handy blade in their bellies? It doesn't work that way, I guess you know. You can't jump halfway through a floor or in a tree. Even if you want. It just doesn't happen. But you've *got* to have a clear spot to land, and you've made that damnably hard to do. They'll have to hit you one or two at a time."

Sister-Major nodded. "That's the idea. One or two at a time's all we can handle."

"I don't have to tell you you were right," he said plainly, "but I will. We've a whole breed of long-jumpers on our hands. I don't know why but we do."

"We'll face what we must," she said calmly. "God hasn't deserted us yet."

He's not helping a great deal, either, Lars said to himself.

* * *

Ham was nowhere in sight, but Sean and Carilee found Will on a level below.

"I guess I'm glad to see you," Will muttered, "though why in hell you came is something else."

"I won't argue that," said Lars. "Does anybody know what's happened to Jeffrey? I hope he's not missing all this. The bastard deserves a front row seat. Is there a chance for food and drink in this place, or have you finished it all off? My belly's so empty I could eat a Churcher pig."

Will shot him a sour look. "How can you think of eatin' at a time like this? God's Witness, you're as mad as ever, Lars. Carilee, you get sick of the lout, you let me know."

"Fine. How about now?" She grinned.

"Saints, girl. . . ." Will looked appalled. "You aiming to give me a stroke right here?"

"I could try, Will Travers. What's the harm in that?"

Will never got to answer. From the stairwell came a cry that chilled the blood. . . .

"Demons . . . demons in the Keep!"

TWENTY-FIVE

Lars heard the quick, sharp explosions of air and then they were on him, wicked blades blooded from the hapless Churchers above. He jumped at once, appeared an instant atop the Keep to draw his sword, then jumped again to the hall below. Obsidian eyes met his—a razored crescent blurred in a furry fist. Lars staggered back, flailed blindly at the demon and disappeared—

—to the top of the stairs

—and back to the roof of the Keep

—then the far end of the hall

—and the sentry-walk outside

—and back to the stairs again

—all in the space of a breath, and each time the demon was there before him, his deadly war-axe hungry for Lar's blood. Once, he saw Carilee by his side. Again, the short burst of a scream met his ears as a Churcher died, the sound cut off in an instant as Lars vanished.

And every time, the ugly warrior was there, half a beat ahead. There were other jumpers about, but he knew with a chill that this one belonged to him.

Lars felt a sudden moment of cold, unreasoning

fear. He'd run from demons before, losing his pursuers in half a dozen jumps. This demon was different. Lars knew instinctively that he'd never let him go. If he didn't kill him this jump he'd surely do it the next—or the one after the one after that. . . .

Desperately, Lars jumped faster and faster. The instant a new image brushed his mind, he replaced it with another. The scenes before him vanished in a blink, flashes of color and motion gone before his eye could send the message to his brain. . . .

The blink became a blur. Motion and color disappeared. Panic caught him up and wrenched a fearful cry from his throat. The sound was lost behind him, rapid slices of a scream left in a hundred different places. . . .

And still the demon was there . . . he could sense its enormous eyes, the cold edge of a blade that wanted his life. . . .

Lars didn't dare stop the thing that he'd begun. In truth, he wasn't certain that he could. He no longer chose his own destinations, he was moving too fast for that. Some other part of his mind had taken the task, a part of his self he didn't know.

It won't work . . . no matter how fast I jump, this devil's a feather-second faster. . . !

Dimly, he became aware of the sound. It climbed the scale, rising to a high, near unbearable pitch. Beside it was its shadow, a sound indistinguishable from the first. Lars knew in an instant that the first sound was himself, and that the second belonged to the demon. The sounds shrieked higher and higher, pressed closer and closer together. He knew in a moment of terror the two would meet, that there was nothing he could do to keep them apart. He tried to flee, to pull himself away. And in that timeless instant, he felt the demon's panic match his own. . . .

His muzzle was damp, the air about him thick with the smell of mold . . . the taste in his mouth held the sweet rank memory of meat, still pleasantly warm with life. . . .

A thought dropped toward him through a viscous pool of oil . . . when it was closer he could see it . . . he remembered the cold, the rain pounding his back and chilling his pelt . . . they'd been waiting half the night and he was stiff and sore all over . . . his head ached, the haft of his axe was heavy as lead . . . when the war-horns finally sounded, he rose up gratefully and howled his killing song. . . .

The squat-bodied bare-faces charged . . . he jumped and cleaved ghostly white flesh clear to the gut . . . jumped again and let his mind sniff out the dull red path . . . followed each treacherous twist and hollow of the ever-shifting lines, his axe seeking the blood of the hairless foe. . . .

A warmer, sleepier thought nudged the others aside . . . he smelled the sharp, exciting scent of her hide, the deep and musky places beneath her fur . . . her padded fingers stroked him, drawing him ever closer, closer and closer still—

Lars shrank back in horror, his mind painting a quick and desperate picture of the Keep. Nothing. He opened his eyes on darkness. He was alone in a black and formless abyss. He tried one image and then another. The barracks. The grove by the stream. There was nothing there but the dark. The dark, and the loneliness that lasted forever.

*Lars—Lars don't leave me out here take me with
you. For God's sake, Lars!*

Who are you? Who's that?

I'm here, Lars . . . right here—please!

Damn you, whoever you are let me go. . . .

NO! No!

Let go of me or I'll—

Lars sat up and stared. Amian stared back, his face
white as paste.

"*Morse!* Where in all hell did *you* come from!"

Amian swallowed air like a fish. "I'm d-damned if *I*
know. . . ."

Carilee cried out and took Lars in her arms. "Lars,
what happened? Praise God you're all right!"

Lars climbed shakily to his feet. His glance took in
the walls. A table. A solid stone floor and the others
standing about. He eased Carilee gently aside, grabbed
Amian's jerkin and pulled him up hard. "We've a
score to settle, friend, but that'll wait. Right now tell
me what the devil you were doing out there, and
where we were. Talk, damn you, and quickly!"

Morse shook his head in desperation. "I told you,
Lars—I don't *know!* Honest to God, I don't. Look,
I'm sorry for what I did. I was wrong and I didn't
think."

"Shut up!" snapped Lars. "You never had a thought
in your miserable life. That's not what I asked, now
is it! I want to know what *happened* out there. . . ."

Morse took a breath. "I followed Carilee and Sean.
I wanted to help, and that's the truth. When we ran
into the demons—" Morse stopped. "I don't *know,*
Lars. I was so bloody scared. I jumped and then—"

"—And then you *kept* jumping right? With a demon on your tail."

Morse looked surprised. "Yeah, that's right. That's—that's exactly what happened."

Lars pushed him roughly aside. "Something damned peculiar's happening here, O'Farr. Besides *him* showing up, I just got caught in a demon's head and I didn't bloody like it."

"You did *what?*"

Lars looked at Morse. "That didn't happen to you, did it? But you got away all the same. Floatin' about in the dark or whatever. And you got there running scared, jumping as fast as you could." Lars frowned. "Where's Sean? Has he brought in the others?"

"They're here," Carilee told him. "He got them as soon as the attack was over. They're atop the Keep. Fighting, but not jumping. I thought that's what you'd want."

"Good. For now it's just as well—" Lars stopped and turned quickly as the clatter of arms and armor sounded in the hall. Will Travers and Ham burst in as a squad of Churcher soldiers raced by.

"This way and fast," snapped Will, "the bastards have broken through and breached the eastern wall. My God, Morse—where'd *you* come from!"

A shout of alarm rose up from below. Lars herded the others out and down the hall. At the stairwell he paused and looked into the chamber below. The sight there set his flesh to crawling. Townsmen and Churchers packed the room in a smothering mass. Swarming through a great rift in the wall was the head of the demon horde, a wedge of dark-furred bodies and iron helms. As Lars watched, the demons surged forward and slashed the Churchers back. Then, the tide turned abruptly and Churchers filled the gap, taking back the bloody inches they'd given away.

"If they're in the Keep we're lost," Will shouted in his ear. "We'll never get the devils out!"

Lars pulled him aside and guided him back to the others. "At least, there's no room for jumpers in such a fight. Where's Sister-Major, do you know?"

"That way," Ham yelled, "up another floor and to yer right!"

"Carilee—jump to the top of the Keep and check on Sean." He shot Morse a warning. "Take Amian with you and give him a blade. You'd best use it well or I'll hear it. And Carilee— When you're finished join me quickly."

Carilee nodded and disappeared.

Lars followed Ham and Will. It was slow going, for the halls and stairs were filled with jumper traps. Sister-Major's command post was a shambles. Wooden tables blocked the door. Timbers webbed the room, and bowmen stood at the ready. Lars and his companions squeezed inside, stopping to let a harried courier pass.

Sister-Major dismissed a captain and turned to Lars. "I just lost Micah," she said grimly. "We tried to get to him but there was no time. Micah, and maybe twenty others."

"I'm sorry," said Lars. "He was a damned good man."

Sister-Major shook her head. "We're losing them too fast to count. We might hold 'em off if that was all. We can't stop the jumpers, Lars Haggart. The traps help—but they're too fast, too deadly. They kill a hundred for every one we stop." She looked over her shoulder and glanced sharply at Lars. "I've sent Holy Mother through the tunnel, down toward the ship. There's a squad of men with her, all I can spare. If something happens to me. . . ."

Lars forced a laugh. "Satan himself couldn't stop you, Sister. He'd be foolish to even try."

Sister-Major thrust out her chin. "And who do you think that *is* out there, Lars Haggart?" Suddenly, her eyes went hard as stone. "It all happened so fast. I was a fool—I should have stopped Jeffrey, seen his cunning sooner. God forgive me, but I pray I find him first before the demons."

Sister-Major started as Carilee appeared. Her face was smeared with soot, and fire had singed her hair.

"They're hitting us hard up there," she said shakily. "Jumpers, trying to drop ropes and ladders for the rest. They've archers with fire arrows, Lars, to set the traps afire. My God—they know where we are, where we're going next. . . ."

"Are you holding?" Sister-Major asked sharply.

"Just barely. I can't say for how long. Lars— Maureen's dead. And Marcus and Sergeant Hale. And—Sean's hurt bad."

"How bad, Carilee?" Her silence told him the answer.

"If it's all right I'll get back. They need everyone they can get."

"I'll try to send help," said Sister-Major. "We *can't* let them take the top of the Keep."

"Carilee, wait—" Lars stopped her. "Get Amian, and come back with him."

"What?"

"Just *do* it, O'Farr, and quickly."

Carilee vanished. Sister-Major gave him a curious look. "What is it, Captain? You look as if you've just seen a ghost."

"I don't know. Maybe I have." *They know where we are, where we're going next. . . .*

Carilee appeared, Amian by her side. Morse gave

Lars a wary glance, as if he'd rather be on the roof fighting demons.

"Amian, forget what's between us and just listen," said Lars. "Something happened out there that's never happened before. We both ran from demons and the chase took us—somewhere else. It wasn't the place I found the Drifters. It was—*closer,* if that makes any sense."

Morse shook his head. "I don't know, Lars. I was just hangin' there in the dark. Hoping they wouldn't find me again."

"You must have seen something, *felt* something...."

"No, I just—"

"Damn it, man, think!" Lars flared. "There's a *reason* those jumpers are getting stronger. I can't say why, but I'm certain it's something to do with what happened to us." He turned quickly from Morse. "You sensed it, Sister-Major. And I saw it happen. When our bowmen attacked the demons they—switched *time* about somehow. Took another path. . . ."

"Lars, wait—" Amian's eyes went wide. "You said— taking another path. . . ."

"What, Morse?"

"I *did* see something, felt it and saw it both. It was all around me, like a— Like a bunch of hummin' lines."

"Go on," urged Lars.

"It was— Yeah, webs, that's it. *Spider* webs, Lars. Webs goin' every which way, red humming webs that take you where you want to go. . . ."

Lars came erect, his heart pounding frantically against his chest. "God's Witness, he's right. I saw it too, and tried to put it out of my head. I was in the demon's thoughts and wanted nothing to do with that." He closed his eyes and frowned. "He was jumping, remembering where he'd been. There was a dull red path—just like Amian said. . . . Twists and turns he had to follow." Lars stopped, opened his eyes and stared. "My God, it's true. . . . It can't be, but it is. . . ."

"Lars, *what?*" asked Carilee.

"It's us," he said flatly. "There wouldn't *be* long-jumpers if it wasn't for us. That's how they do it. They *home in* on the Karma Corps. Every one of us is some kind of a—beacon. They can smell us, damn 'em—sniff us out wherever we are. The webs are paths that lead right to us. The more they attack us the stronger they get, and the better the paths become."

"That doesn't explain what happened to me," said Morse.

"Use your head for once," Lars said sharply. "It explains exactly what happened. You jumped, and instead of landing where you wanted you got caught in one of the paths, then tossed off into the dark. It never happened before because—hell, I don't know, maybe because the paths weren't strong enough then for *us* to sense 'em. Right—that makes sense. When the demon came after me, our paths came so close to being the same, we wound up in each other's heads." Lars made a face. "I don't *ever* want to do that again."

He was aware, then, that the sounds of battle had quieted. "It happens," said Sister-Major. "They've pulled off for the moment. They'll be back."

"To finish us off, no doubt," Morse grumbled.

Lars turned and grasped Carilee's hands. "You're in command, O'Farr. For God's sake, don't jump if you can help it. Our talents only mark us all the better."

"And where'll *you* be then? If I—" Carilee's eyes went wide. "No, now you *can't*. You mustn't even think it, Lars Haggart!"

"What else would you have me do?" he said gently. "The answer's out there, not here. If we don't find it soon, there'll be no use in the search." He turned and let his eyes touch Morse. "You're the only other who knows the way. Will you come with me or not?"

Amian's face went white. "Lars, I'd—I'd be no good to you there. I truly wouldn't. . . ."

There was no anger at all in Lars' eyes. To Morse, there was something to see far worse than that. "Then I'd not have you with me," he said. With a last quick look at Carilee, he closed his eyes and vanished.

TWENTY-SIX

Lars could see nothing at all, but he sensed that something was there. It was a darkness with form and shape, a shadow-world that had no use for light. Strangely, he didn't fear the dark. It was the natural state of the place, the way it was meant to be. It was the *silence* that chilled his blood, for he knew the faintest of whispers had never intruded here.

Lars became dimly aware of a pale, luminous glow against the dark. As he watched it came again, like distant summer lightning in a storm. In the blink of an eye the light grew larger—as if he'd jumped to the source, or the source had come to him. He knew, then; simply thinking about the light brought it nearer.

Cautiously, he thought himself closer, and closer still. . . .

Suddenly, shimmering color was all around him, pulsing red lines that turned and twisted upon themselves, vanished and disappeared and appeared again in a constantly changing pattern. . . .

Careful, careful . . . danger!

Lars backed off, letting the lines fade to a respectful distance. He knew what they were, and why there was danger here. He'd found the demon paths.

This was the thing he'd seen when he touched the other's mind. Amian had seen it too—webs of power tucked between the worlds, webs that led the demon jumpers to their prey.

Lars felt suddenly helpless. He could float in this dark and nether place forever, between one heartbeat and the next. God's Mercy, this was the demon's land, not his! What good did a pathway do if a man was blind and lame!

Use it, use it . . . the path is there, Lars Haggart . . . it's yours, as well as any other's. . . .

No, it's not mine at all . . . I'm a man, not a bloody imp!

Feel it . . . let the web take you where it will. . . .

And who the hell are you? You know so much, you do it, friend!

Careful, Lars . . . careful. . . .

What? What's that!

They're coming, Lars . . . now they know you're here. . . .

Suddenly, he could feel them all around him, sense their terrible anger and almost hear their demon howls. The dark about was thick with flitting ghosts, pale shadows of warriors all too real. They sliced with spectral swords, cleaved with phantom axe and scythe. His flesh had no more substance than their blades, but the assault was no less chilling. In some far corner of his mind, Lars Haggart knew there were wounds a man could take in this dark place far worse than any other—wounds that cut to the soul and never healed.

Fight them, Lars, fight them . . . make for the way!

With a burst of anger none could hear, Lars struck back with a vengeance, slashing again and again at wraithlike bone and armor. Shards of light exploded and disappeared. The circle widened about him. Lars swung his blade in a killing arc, forcing the demons back, and back again. . . .

The path, Lars . . . find the path and hold it!

Whoever you are, friend, you hold it . . . I've all I can handle here. . . .

Take the path, Lars, take it. . . .

All right, damn it, all right!

Lars struck out again with savage fury, cutting his way ever closer to the lancing beams of power. The demon shades seemed to sense what he was after. Of a sudden, a hundred phantom warriors joined the fray, and then a hundred more. Lars fought desperately for ground. The pale edge of his blade scattered smoke. The demons pressed him steadily back, farther and farther from the path. Lars knew it was over, that he couldn't take them all, couldn't hold them a moment longer. . . .

Suddenly, a greater brightness than the phantoms pressed about him caught his eye. It danced in and out of his vision, shrinking back for the moment, then sparking forth again. Then, at once, with an angry surge of power, it burst through the warrior wraiths, scattering blossoms of fire.

"*Looks to me like you could use an extra blade, Captain. Mind if I lend a hand?*"

"*Amian! What the devil are you doing here!*"

"*What I should've been doin' all along, Lars Haggart—standing by your side 'stead of causing you harm and trouble. You're right as rain, Captain—thinkin' too hard's my undoing.*"

"*Well I'm glad you thought of this—hold there, and take my right. Make for the path!*"

Amian moved to his side, a sheet of bright blue

flame that matched his own fiery image. Together, they met the demon horde, lashed out relentlessly at ghostly armor and iron.

"Take them, Morse . . . press on, press on!"

"To your left, Captain—have a care!"

At once, Lars felt a sudden surge of power, a wondrous understanding of this place between the worlds. In an instant, he knew the subtle pulse of time, knew as if he'd always known before why a demon was a hair-second faster, a killing moment ahead. Now, he and Amian shared that power; they could meet and match the imps, face them on equal ground. Lars knew he'd passed this way a thousand times before, that every jump took him here but for an instant. No longer was he a stranger, an intruder passing through. His nether mind and body were as one with the ever-shifting paths, the lightning webs of power. Though the demons had found it first, Lars had guessed the truth: It was the presence of his own good folk that had shown the way. The demons were jumpers and nothing more. They were the strangers here, not the Karma Corps. They'd sensed the strength of Lars and his own, and turned that strength against them. . . .

Even as his thoughts took shape, the demon hordes stirred. They sparked the fiery paths, singed the dark with their anger.

"They're afraid, Amian . . . we've found their secret and they don't much like it. . . . Get back now— bring the Corps here, all of them and quickly. We'll send them through the path and back to Citadel—see how the bastards like fightin' blades as fast as theirs. Tell Carilee she—"

"Holy God, Lars, what's that?"

Lars felt it, too—a cold, unreasoning fear that

lashed out and ripped at the core of his soul. He shrank back instinctively, fighting the urge to flee.

"Lars!"

"Hold, Amian, hold. . . ."

"I can't, Lars . . . there's something out there, something bloody awful!"

Lars knew it at once. He'd met the thing before, when he and Will had tried to jump back to their green beside the river. It had been there then, its terrible presence blocking their way.

"Take it easy, Morse, I know what it is . . . it wants to stop us, keep us from going farther. . . ."

"Good, that's fine with me. Lars, we've got what we came for—we know how to fight 'em. . . ."

"Then what's that thing trying to hide? What, Amian?"

"I don't care, Lars. God's Mercy, come on!"

"Wait . . . wait. . . ."

"Captain, they're dying in Citadel, our folk and the others. If you won't show them the way, I will—"

"Morse, no!" In that instant he felt the fearful presence loom larger, sensed its frigid breath. *"Morse, my God don't bring them here!"* Too late. The nether form beside him disappeared.

He was alone.

Only the other was there.

He knew, now, exactly what it wanted. Every blessed soul it could get. . . . And Amian Morse was about to deliver the whole Corps into its hands. . . .

"No damn you, I won't let you have them!"

With the sudden calm of desperation, Lars jumped his phantom self into the thing he couldn't see. . . .

Lars Haggart screamed forever. . . .

He was falling, tumbling through a darkness he knew would never end. He was no longer afraid.

Fear was an intruder, a shadow-thing that crouched in the dark and made faces. The fear he knew now was inside looking out.

Lars, listen—listen to me, man!

Who's that? You were here before. . . .

It's Will Travers, you fool. Who'd you think it was?

No—oh, no, it's a trick. . . . Will doesn't have the power, all he can do is dream.

Don't tell me what I can do and what I can't . . . I'm learning fast, Lars, and you'd damn well better do the same. . . .

Lars, listen to him, please. Will's trying to help!

Carilee? God's Mercy, it's got you too!

Nothing's got us, Lars . . . .

We're all here. . . .

All of us. . . .

Every one. . . . Right here. . . .

Let Will help. . . . Listen, Lars. . . .

Listen, Lars, listen. . . .

All of you? The—the whole Corps? Will, you've doomed them all—you and that fool Amian Morse! God, I told him to keep them away. Sister-Major's right—there is a hell, and we're all headed straight for the bottom!

Shut up, boy, and listen. There's no damned presence, and no hell either. It's fear, Lars—nothing more than that. The demons' fear and ours; whoever find the way, and wants to go beyond. That's all it is, Lars.

And you're mad as an owl, Will Travers—it's a trap, and we stepped right in it. . . .

Listen, Lars . . . listen carefully, now. It's a trap, but not the kind you think. Once they saw you'd found the way, the demons let you seize the path.

You've got the power, Lars—only it won't do you a bloody bit of good. . . .

Will, stop it! If you hadn't doomed us all we could have faced the bastards as equals.

Never equals, Lars. That's what they wanted you to think, why they let you have it. They fooled me too or I'd never have urged you on. The power's not enough. They know the paths too well . . . we don't have time to learn to beat 'em. They'd always be a second faster . . . always a step ahead . . .

No, that's a lie!

Lars, you've got to listen to Will!

Damn me, Carilee—I've got the rest of forever to listen to Will. . . .

You listen, but you don't hear, Lars. The thing that's got you now is only fear. . . . The demons are a lot more frightened of it than you. Lars—they let you find the paths, let you think you'd won the prize. So you'd run back and share it with the Corps, thinking you had the strength to fight them. . . .

I would have, too—if you hadn't let them all into the pit . . . !

I'm not in your damned pit, Lars—and neither is anyone else. The rest of the Corps is free. . . .

What? What!

I took them right through that wall of fear, and brought them out again. Taught 'em how to do what they need to do. If you'll shut up and listen, I'll teach you, too—

Ah, fine. The man with no power but dreamin' is going to drag me out of hell. . . .

It's true, Lars. That's what I was, but I'm not anymore. You took care of that. The instant you disappeared, my old head damn near exploded. I saw where you were and what you were doing, and I knew all at once what I was. I'm a pathfinder, Lars, I know where things are supposed to be, and how to find 'em . . .

But—why, Will? You say you brought the Corps down here, down into the dark!

Because it's the right way to go, Lars Haggart. What you don't know, boy, is you stuck your nose where it didn't belong and found the answer. That's where the real power is—right beyond a wall of fear—where else? The demons wouldn't go near it, but you did!

God, if you're lyin' to me, old man. . . .

Would I lie about knowing the clear road to other worlds? To the green beside the river, the place where you were born? The way to the Drifter place, how to free John-William and the rest? Stars you've never seen, and every yesterday and tomorrow you've ever imagined?

Damn it all, get me out of here, Will!

Listen, Lars, we were right from the beginning. Jumping where you like's a way of being—not doing. If you try too hard you never make it. You've got to stop fighting, that's the secret. Jumping in and out of time or 'cross the room is all the same. Stop being afraid of what's there, waiting behind something you've never seen. That's why drunks and dreamers go dashing about, Lars Haggart. They're not thinking at all, they're just being . . . you can't do it, you've got to be. . . .

Help me, Will. . . .

I'm helping, Lars. . . .

We all are, Lars. . . .

I'm—trying. . . .

Stop, damn it—trying isn't it!

Right, right. . . .

Be, Lars . . . be where you want to be. . . .
Be . . . yes. . . .
Be there . . . feel . . . know it's true. . . .
Yes. . . .
*The paths belong to you . . . everywhere you want
is yours . . . Yes . . . yes!*
Come to us, Lars . . . Be there . . .
Everywhere . . .
Be here . . . be here now . . .
Now, Lars . . .
NOW!

"Lars, Oh, Lars, you did it!"

"Carilee, Will! You're all here—all of you!"

"And wastin' time we are, too," growled Morse. "We've got some fightin' to do, and I say we get right at it."

Sister-Major Celeste caught her breath and listened. She knew the sounds of battle; she could read them as well as a book. The sounds that reached her now were nothing at all like those of a moment before. Grasping the hilt of her sword, she moved rapidly toward the door. Before she reached the barricade, a young lieutenant slipped inside, caught her sleeve and held her.

"Damn your insolence, what is it?" She jerked free and glared. "Speak up, Joshua!"

The lad tried, but his mouth refused to work. Sister-Major pushed him aside and made her way across the hall. Whatever it was, she thought darkly, it had to be more bad news. The demons were fair crawling out of the walls, and there was nothing more she could do. Only Heaven's hand could stop them now.

More than that, not half a minute before, Lars Haggart had disappeared. Ten seconds after, the coward Amian Morse had vanished as well, returned near as fast as he'd gone, screamed at the girl and vanished again with the whole bloody lot. Maybe they'd gone for good. She didn't think Lars Haggart would desert her, but how could she fault him if he did? Staying here would only—

Sister-Major stopped short at the top of the stairs, blinked and shook her head to clear her eyes. Everywhere she looked, demon jumpers were dying, dropping their weapons and falling limply to the floor! It was as if God Himself had struck them down, for no mortal hand had touched them at all. Before she could blink again, a dozen more fell, then twice that and a hundred, and then a hundred more. . . .

From the growing dark below, a great shout rose up from weary troops. As a man, they leaped their barricades and charged, straight at the demon ranks. Sister-Major bellowed an order, rallying troops to her from every point of the Citadel.

The bulk of the demon army had driven clear to the walls of the Keep, pressing the Churchers back and letting their jumpers make the way. Now, the jumpers were suddenly gone, those who couldn't vanish slain in seconds before their eyes. For a breathless moment more the demons held, still determined to take the warriors of Mother Church.

Then, even as they met and closed with the foe, demons within the horde began to twist in the throes of death and fall away, cut down as quickly as their jumpers moments before. Neither blade nor arrow were seen, only rapid whispers of light moving grimly through their ranks. Wherever the light touched another died, and then another. A ripple of fear swept through the army like a wind, from the demons facing the foe in Citadel, to the thousands massed outside, hungry for the kill. For an instant the army held, then as if some cold and wintry breath had touched them all they turned and fled, leaving a sea of blood-red pennons and iron weapons in their wake. . . .

EPILOGUE

He'd watched them from the battlement atop the Keep, waited as a dawn as red as blood began to taint the ruined ground. Half a league away, past the town beyond the bounds of Citadel they stood in silence, thousands upon thousands, as far as the eye could see. Some still wore a bit of tattered iron armor, a studded copper helm that caught the sun. They watched the Keep with black obsidian eyes, dark-furred figures still as death.

"It's enough to chill yer blood," said Ham, his voice scarce a whisper. "God's Holy Eyes, what a sight."

"I'm frightened of them still," said Carilee. "I can't help it, Lars."

"It's all right," Lars told her, clutching her ice-cold hand within his own. "It's all over now."

"They're waiting for something," said Sister-Major. "What do they want, Lars Haggart? What are they waiting *for?*"

"They're waiting for me," said Lars. . . .

He saw the other at once, a phantom wisp against the dark. All around them, the paths of power flickered in an ever-shifting pattern.

"I guessed that we could speak," said Lars, "that there'd be no barriers between us."

"We can speak," said the demon. "There are no tongues here, only one mind touching another."

"You're the one. Our minds have met before."

"I'm the one, though I'd wish it was another. It's my shame that I led you to a power we didn't imagine!"

"Don't blame yourself for that. The fighting's at an end; the victory's yours as well as ours. . . ."

The demon didn't answer. Lars could sense the tension in the nether figure before him, wire-thin veins of lightning that danced upon his flesh. "Who are you?" he demanded. "What are you? You're like the bare-faces, yet you're not the same at all. You have the power, stronger and more frightening than we ever imagined it could be. Why do you fight for them? They used you to kill—even we could see that!"

Lars watched the fiery tints of anger slowly fade. "I could ask you the same and I will. Why did you fight the Churchers? What in hell did you want? You had the whole bloody world, and they'd nothing but a dirty little corner. What's the good of that to you? Damn me, did you have to have it all!"

Once more, the phantom figure blazed, this time in a cobalt flame of disbelief. "You—you truly don't know? No, I can see it. . . . you speak the truth. . . . You don't know at all!"

"What? What is it I don't know, demon?"

"They didn't tell you. They didn't tell you what they did to us. . . ."

Lars looked up and saw her gaunt figure striding toward him across the yard. She walked stiff as a board, as if the whole Churcher army were massed behind her. He smiled and leaned back, letting the sun warm his face. Even without a war to fight, she was still the Sister-Major.

"A cup of ale, Sister? I've a good jug cooling inside."

"I didn't come for drink," she said tightly, "I came for talk, Lars Haggart. Ham said you were here, that you— Damn you, Captain, you know I've been waiting half the day. You could have come to *me*."

"I needed a little time, Sister-Major."

"A little time for what?"

"To sort things out, get my head in order."

"Huh! I'm not surprised, I guess. It's a blessed wonder you've still got your senses. Speaking to Satan's imps, just like they were—God's own creatures!"

"You're going to have to come to it," he said calmly. "Either now or later. They're not Satan's imps, just folk like any other."

Sister-Major caught her breath. "God help you, Lars Haggart—they've put you under a spell!"

"No spells, Sister. Just talk. Sit down and let me bring you a mug of ale. A *large* mug, I'd say, to hear what I have to tell."

Sister-Major shook her head. "Get on with it. What gibberish did the demon put in your head?"

"He told me what the war was all about—why they've fought you two hundred years, and would have gladly fought you two hundred more. It's the ship, Sister-Major. They wanted the ship that's buried 'neath Citadel. . . ."

"*What!*" Sister-Major stared. "But the ship's not—"

"—The ship's no good at all," Lars finished. "We know that, but the demons didn't. All they knew was that *you* had a ship, and they didn't. That you kept it hidden from sight."

"That's—nonsense," she scoffed. "What would Satan's demons want with a ship—even one that *wasn't* ruined and gutted?"

"Nothing. If imps were all they were. They're not, though, whatever you wish to believe. They're folk from another world, the same as you. Or at least, their fathers' fathers were. They wanted your ship, Sister, because they wanted to get back home. Home's not just a world to them, it's something more. It's a—part of what they are. They're not—whole, complete, without it. They'd do anything to get there— anything at all."

Lars paused a moment, fingering the rim of his mug. "There's something your bloody ancestors didn't tell you, Sister-Major. There was another ship here, circling this world when you arrived. Holy *missionaries* or not your ship was armed, and the other wasn't. The Good Brothers and Sisters brought it down without a warning, using some weapon of awesome strength. It may be that's what caused your lovely vessel to lose its power, to ruin its magical engines and send it to ground. The other ship came down as well, half the folk aboard it dead. And when they learned your people were here. . . ."

"Holy *God*, Lars Haggart!" Sister-Major shook, her face mottled with anger. "If you—*believe* this demon's tale, why you're a fool. It's Satan's words he's put in your head!"

"Is it?" Lars said quietly. "And why do you think he'd tell me such a thing? What's the good of it, Sister? The war's over and done, the fight here's finished. Why tell me anything at all?"

Sister-Major rose calmly, and gathered her robes

about her. Her eyes betrayed nothing at all, but Lars had come to know her, and saw a great deal more than she wished him to see. "We'll talk another time, Lars Haggart. When you've come to your senses again. I'm certain a merciful God will bring you to reason. . . ."

Without another word, she turned and walked across the yard and through the gate. Lars watched until a hot summer wind raised a whirl of sand and blocked her from sight.

"You think she believes you, Lars? It doesn't seem to *me* she does."

"Ah, I thought it might be you," Lars said without turning. "Have you no shame at all, Carilee? Lurking behind doors and filling your ears?"

"I wasn't *lurking* behind a door. I was upstairs in the loft." She brushed gently past him and set her ale upon the table. The sun sparked green in her eyes, and the breeze pressed amber hair across her cheek.

"It's a strange tale, Lars. And her being a Churcher and all."

"She'll have to believe it in time," said Lars. "She's a Churcher like you say, but she's a mind as keen as a blade for all of that. Even Mother Church hasn't managed to stop her from thinking." He raised a curious brow at Carilee. "I see that *you* find all this easy enough to swallow. It's a fair wondrous tale, you'll have to admit."

"I can tell your *wondrous* tales from the others," she said coolly. "God knows I've had the practice."

"And what would you say was wondrous and what was not?" he asked, knowing of a sudden he was treading dangerous ground.

"Oh, tales of ravished Virgin Mothers and such as that."

"And which would you say that was? A yarn or something else?"

"Something else," she said with a shrug. "You're innocent of that. Just barely, though."

"That's a blessed relief."

"Don't you want to know *why?*" She showed him a cunning smile. "How is it I know what you did and didn't do?"

"God's Truth, girl, I don't *care* why, as long as it's done."

Carilee laughed. "You'll think upon it, though."

"Damned if I will," he said tightly, knowing, of course, that she was right. A picture of raven hair and lips too soft to be imagined touched his thoughts, and he quickly chased it away.

And what's to become of you, then, Anne Marie? This world can never again be what it was. And you can't be a child, not when you've found the woman in yourself. . . .

"Oh, I near forgot," said Carilee. "Amian and Will came back from Citadel. The Churchers found Jeffrey. In a chamber in the Keep. The demons didn't get him; his own men hung him from the rafters."

His own men or another, thought Lars. "There's justice in that," he said. "I can't say that I'm sorry."

Carilee sipped her ale, and wiped a dainty hand across her lips. "You're right, you know. About Sister-Major. She'll brood about it all but she'll be back. Even when she *does* come to reason about the demons, she'll have to come to you for the rest."

"And what would that be, then?"

"The part that *I* can't fathom, either," she said shortly. "I am *not* going to beg you for an answer, Lars Haggart."

Lars grinned. "Demon jumpers, you mean. . . ."

"Of course that's what I mean. It's too much to swallow, and you can bet *she* won't let it go, either. We're jumpers, and some of them have the talent as well. It didn't just *happen* that way, now did it?"

"No," said Lars, "it didn't." He squinted past her at the sun. "The fellow I talked to there. . . . He said it's a harder talent for them. They can pass the skill along, but not to many. Carilee, it seems they've Drifters out there, too. We'll have to help with that. They lose a lot more than they're able to teach. If the talent doesn't take."

"That's not what I asked, now is it?" she persisted.

Lars reached out and took her hand. "Brother Jerome brought us here with ancient magic—something he made from the ship, at a guess. Whatever force that was, Carilee, he gave it to the demons as well."

"What!" She jerked her hand away and stared. "Sister-Major's right, you *have* lost your reason. Jerome brought us here less than two years past. The demons have had jumpers two *centuries!*"

"I know that, O'Farr. I can't prove what I'm saying, but I'm next to certain I'm right. Playing with time's a tricky thing at best. You went with Will to get John-William and the rest, did you not? Ask him, or one of the others. When you're Drifting, no time passes at all. I was there and I felt it. But to poor John-William, it seemed an eternity long. Now which of us is right?"

"I know, but—"

"Something happened. I can't say what it was. When Jerome pulled us out of another world, the power of our passage touched the demons. Only not now—*then*. Two-hundred years in the past." Lars shook his head. "There's a fair irony in that, is there

not? He brought us here to fight the demon jumpers—
the jumpers he made himself. How else could it be,
Carilee? You said it yourself. Would you rather believe
the odds of two folk on a single world—and both of
'em just *happen* to have the power?"

"I'd rather not think about it at all. Doing things
now that happened before they happened—'cause
you *made* 'em happen in the first place. . . ." Carilee
made a face.

"He's dead," said Lars, almost to himself. "That's
how it has to be. He worked such wondrous magic,
yet no one ever wants to speak his name. Now why
is that, I wonder? He guessed the thing he'd done,
Carilee, and couldn't bear to live with that. He's
dead, and the Good Brothers and Sisters of Mother
Church never knew the reason why."

"They won't, either. Unless you tell them."

Lars stood and brought her to her feet and placed
his hands about her waist. "Now why would I do
that? I'm not a thoughtless man, Carilee. You well
know my only joy in life is bringing happiness to
others. Such as yourself, for fair example. . . ."

"I think I'm going to be sick," said Carilee.

"Not yet you're not," Lars told her. "I need you to
fetch Good Will, our famous finder of paths to nether
places. We've a world to find for our impish friends,
and God knows such a task could take the day."

"And if it doesn't, then?"

Lars caught the glint of emerald eyes, that odd tilt
of her head that once again reminded him of a fox.
"It matters not at all, now does it? There's a green by
a river I want you to know. It'll be there still, at the
end of whatever day we wish it to be . . . !"